D0502574

Yulie Paschkis art—Uncle Sam on bike

This book is one of fifteen awarded as part of

the 2007 **We the People Bookshelf** on the **Pursuit of Happiness**

Presented by the National Endowment for the Humanities (NEH) in cooperation with the American Library Association (ALA). NEH and ALA gratefully acknowledge support from Scholastic Inc. for the 2007 Bookshelf.

www.neh.gov **www.ala.org**

My Name Is America

The Journal of Wong Ming-Chung

A Chinese Miner

BY LAURENCE YEP

Scholastic Inc.

New York   Toronto   London   Auckland   Sydney
Mexico City   New Delhi   Hong Kong   Buenos Aires

China
1851

Eighth Month,
Year One of the Era, Prosperity for All

October 1, 1851
Tiger Rock, Southern China

Great news! My uncle, Precious Stone, has announced he is going to the Golden Mountain, or America, as the natives call it. Gold was found there almost three years ago. Many Chinese have already crossed the great ocean to become guests of the Golden Mountain.

So Uncle will make the trip. Then we can eat meat every day instead of once a year at New Year's. And the meat will be prime cut instead of the fat and gristle we usually get. And we'll own five fields like a great family, not two. He's got many plans for when we are rich.

The clan doesn't think much of Uncle. Though Father is younger than Uncle, he actually runs things. The clan thinks Uncle is only clever at knocking scraps of wood together into shelves or little boxes. Worse, they claim he has no luck. They say that if Uncle stood among a thousand people and a cloud drifted overhead, the cloud would rain only on poor Uncle.

I know Uncle is a great man. I'm the only one he can

talk to. Maybe because most people don't think much of me, either. My parents had several children, but only my brother and I lived for very long. And I barely made it. Though my name is Bright Intelligence, everyone calls me Runt. I guess it's because I'm so small.

All great families and great men have chronicles of their achievements. For the sake of future generations, I have begun this diary. And in honor of Uncle's journey, I will record events by both the American and the Chinese calendars.

That's thanks to my teacher, who has an American calendar. Americans do not number their years from the year a ruler comes to power. Perhaps that's because they have no emperor. Nor do their rulers give a name to the era of their rule as ours do.

Another odd thing: Americans measure the year by the sun rather than the moon. So their months don't match the Chinese ones. And their year is fixed at 365 days with an extra one thrown in every four years. It's so rigid. The Chinese calendar can grow large or squeeze small like a living thing.

I rubbed the extra ink stick in the water in the inkwell to make the ink thick for these first pages. And . . .

Well, this chronicle of Uncle's exploits will have to wait. Mother's calling me to wash the rice. It's Blessing's turn but he's disappeared as usual. Though he is fifteen, five years older than me, I wind up doing most of the chores.

October 2

Father is against the idea. He says that none of Uncle's schemes ever work. There was never a blue sky Father couldn't find a cloud in.

Father went to town today just to ask questions. He came back with a bushel basketful of dangers. I didn't know so many men die during the trip. Even more die once they get there.

Uncle tried to argue that it is just as risky staying here. I agree with him. Between taxes and the rent on our other three fields, we barely have enough to eat in a good year. And most of the years have been awful. We once had a drought that lasted for three years. Though the rains came this year, they also brought wars and rebellions over China. Between the soldiers, the rebels, and the bandits, it's hard to keep your head, let alone your food. And the barbarian Manchus, who rule China, keep loading us with more and more taxes to pay for fighting their enemies. The new emperor has chosen "Prosperity for All" as the name for his reign. The prosperity must all belong to him in his palace, because there is no sign of it for common folk like us.

Uncle has to go. He's our only hope.

October 3

I wish my parents would leave Uncle alone. They and the clan keep saying mean things to him. He's hopeless. He's stupid. As they keep at him, he's looking less and less sure. And more and more sad. I think he's starting to believe what they think about him.

When I began this diary, Uncle seemed so tall. However, day by day the clan is shrinking him down to my puny size.

October 4

When I got home from school today, Uncle was all alone in the house with his head in his hands. He looked in such pain that I thought he had cut himself somewhere.

But the pain was all inside. Father and the clan had done their work. They'd convinced Uncle that he had only a thimbleful of luck. And to get to the Golden Mountain, you need a river of it.

I hated to see him so miserable. So I told him to spin backward to change his luck.

"Spin around, turn around, luck changes," he said. He

spun around on one foot and then spread his arms. "There. I've shed the bad luck."

It cheered him up a little.

October 6

I can still hear Uncle and Father arguing in my parents' bedroom. (By rights, the bedroom belongs to Uncle, but he's kind. Instead, he sleeps out in the family room with Blessing and me.)

Father found out what the ticket would cost. It's so much! It would take years and years of good rice harvests to pay for it.

The usual way is to have a merchant buy the ticket for you. When you get overseas, you work off your debt. Because of the interest, it can take eight to ten years.

Uncle, though, wants to be his own man over there, so he told us he is going to sell one of our two fields. Of course, Father was horrified. It shocked even me. As miserable as our two fields are, you never sell land.

I'm no longer sure Uncle is right. Land is everything.

However, as the eldest, Uncle Stone is the head of the family. His word is law.

◈ ◈ ◈

October 8

Uncle left this morning to sell the field and buy his ticket.

At school, I asked my teacher how far it is to the land of the Golden Mountain.

He hemmed and hawed and quoted from the *Classic of Mountains and Seas*. However, one of the guest boys knew. His father went to America the same year gold was found there. It is officially 10,447 kilometers between Shanghai and an American city called Los Angeles.

My teacher used it as a practical arithmetic problem. We had to work it out in American miles. I got the answer first. Even the guest boys with their fancy desks and inks and brushes couldn't beat me. It was something like 6,493 miles.

My teacher seemed surprised I had gotten an answer right. However, I didn't enjoy the glory long before the numbers sank in. I didn't think the whole world was that big, let alone an ocean.

When I asked my teacher how long the voyage would take, he couldn't give me a definite answer. It depends on the winds that blow against the ship's sails. It could be two or even three months.

So we would remember what really counts in life, he had us recite his favorite proverb: "Stinking money, fragrant ink."

It means that it is better to be a scholar than a merchant. A scholar uses perfumed ink, whereas a merchant handles filthy money.

Even so, the wealth of the guest boys keeps them safe from our teacher's bamboo rod. Will it protect us soon?

Later

Until now, I have always envied those boys like Piggy. Guest boys live in fancy houses. Piggy knows all the latest tunes because his family is always visiting the district capital. They eat only the best foods.

Piggy can buy any book he wants. He reads all the time instead of doing chores. Best of all, Piggy and the guest boys don't have to leave during harvest season to work in the fields. The rest of us do. Then we have to study harder to catch up.

It's almost like they're living in a fairy tale.

In a way they are, because in fairy tales, the heroes are always brave and risk great dangers like the guests have done. And in the end, they live happily ever after.

Once Uncle is a guest, we'll be able to stay in school all the time.

My brother hates that idea. He hates studying. In fact, he's had to repeat several levels already. I've caught up to him, so now we use the same textbook.

He says he wants to go with Uncle. He'll do anything to get out of homework and chores.

October 18

Father, Mother, and Uncle have argued ever since Uncle got back. They say it's not too late to get a refund on his ticket. Uncle is standing his ground.

For once, the clan treats him with respect. Our whole family has gotten some. My teacher has even stopped beating me.

Most of the time I am his target. He doesn't dare strike the guest boys if they act up. They are too rich, and the school depends on their donations. So he makes his point by whipping poor boys like me.

Today, though, he told me that he knows a good carpenter who could make new desks for my brother and me. He also knows a good ink maker. When my uncle reaches the Golden Mountain, I should stop using these cheap ink sticks. All the guest boys use ink sticks that have perfume mixed in with the ink.

I promised to ask for his references when Uncle reaches America.

◈ ◈ ◈

October 22

Just got back this evening after a walk with Uncle. I went with him as he said his good-byes. Blessing tagged along, too.

The landlord's son, Lucky, has decided to go along, as well as a cousin named Virtue. They act as if they had the idea first rather than Uncle. From the way the clan fawns over them, you'd think Uncle had dropped off the face of the earth. Uncle doesn't seem to care. We left them bragging about the fist-sized nuggets they would bring back.

Blessing, Uncle, and I walked out the village gates. The fields had been freshly manured. I held my nose, but Uncle inhaled as if it were incense.

He walked from field to field and tree to tree and along the stream. He was saying farewell not to people but to our valley.

I was getting bored. Blessing got more and more fidgety. I couldn't understand why.

We climbed with Uncle to the mouth of the valley. Tiger Rock stood guard there. Centuries ago, a tiger was said to have led our first ancestor into this valley. Then it changed to stone to protect him. Over the centuries it had helped the clan fight off its enemies.

Uncle patted the tiger's head. People from the clan do that when they want good luck. After a thousand years

11

of rubbing, one side of the head is smoother and smaller than the other.

Then Uncle gazed toward the next valley. I realized I didn't know what was beyond that. Another valley? And maybe another and another? Until you reached the great ocean?

Suddenly, the world seemed so huge that I felt as tiny as a bug.

Uncle told me that he has never been beyond the market town. I haven't been even that far.

I told him how far the Golden Mountain is.

Uncle looked a little afraid. "That far?"

I remembered what father had said at dinner. "It's not too late to change your mind."

Uncle thought about it, then shook his head. He has no wife and no children. He has been nowhere and done nothing. This is his one and only chance. For himself. For the family.

I was never prouder of Uncle than at that moment.

Suddenly, Blessing got on his knees and bowed formally to Uncle.

I guess my brother had been working up his courage to that moment. Blessing begged Uncle to take him with him. After all, he is the head of the family and could order Blessing to go.

Uncle turned him down politely. When he gets rich,

he said, he'll send for Blessing to help pick up all those gold nuggets. He isn't going to bother with any fist-sized nuggets like Lucky and Virtue. He is going to pick up only the melon-sized ones.

Blessing said that if he was my size, he would stow away in Uncle's basket.

I thought of that big, big world outside. Then I patted the tiger's head. I like our valley. I'm going to stay here forever with my books.

October 23

It was a regular parade when Uncle, Lucky, and Virtue left.

The clan lined either side of the street. "Good luck! Good luck!" they called.

Lucky led Uncle and Virtue toward the gates. He strutted like a rooster. He's the smartest in the clan. Everyone is sure Lucky's going to come back rich.

Virtue promised his wife and children that he'll send back necklaces of gold nuggets so big they won't be able to walk. Everyone believes him, too, because he's the strongest.

Uncle just walked humbly in their shadows. We escorted him as far as the village gates. Then my family climbed the walls to watch the group leave. They walked along the dikes through the rice fields. The sun was so bright they seemed like paper cutouts.

Father shaded his eyes to watch. I'd never seen him so sad. He looked as if he were mourning already.

I guess I was wrong when I thought Father was just being mean to Uncle. I suppose Father was really trying to keep Uncle alive.

I miss Uncle already. He is always cheerful, finding reasons for everyone to smile. If a windstorm flattened the rice, he would say that at least it was good kite weather.

What will happen to Uncle? And what will happen to us?

◇ ◇ ◇

Ninth and Tenth Months,
Year One of the Era, Prosperity for All

November 1

On the way to school, Blessing grumbled that the waiting is the hardest.

I started to agree with him, but then Piggy said that this is going to be the easiest bet he has ever won. It seems that they have made a wager on Uncle.

Piggy told us the odds are already eight to one.

Piggy has plenty of money for his allowance, but I knew Blessing didn't have any money, so I asked him what he had risked.

It turns out that Blessing has staked me.

I got mad because he can't treat me like a slave. Blessing just laughed. His laugh is a lot like Uncle's. If he loses, I will have to let Piggy copy my homework for a month. Blessing was pleased with his cleverness. He slapped me on the back because my book learning was finally good for something.

How could I refuse after all the times he protected me against the bigger boys?

More than ever I wanted Uncle to reach the Golden Mountain. Not just for the money. I want to see Piggy's face when he has to pay up.

November 11

The odds are twelve to one now. The other guest boys are getting into the bet. It will be bad enough to hear that Uncle is dead, but I will also be doing other people's homework for the rest of my life.

November 13

The other night Blessing surprised me. Usually he's asleep as soon as we lie down on our sleeping mats. He asked me if I had read anything about the Golden Mountain in any book.

I said I hadn't but he could check the geography books in our teacher's little library. Blessing hemmed and hawed at first, but finally confessed that the words might be too hard. Could I help him?

If I hadn't been lying down already, I would have fallen over. He is the strong, handsome one. I am just the runt. I am always the one who has to come to him for favors.

Blessing said that he thought the Golden Mountain

would shine in the sun. It would be so bright, you'd have to squint.

I'd never heard him talk like that. Usually he's tough, but his voice was all soft and dreamy.

I did my best today. No luck, though. I couldn't find anything on the Golden Mountain.

He looks so disappointed.

November 16

It's strange. I never knew Blessing had an imagination. For the last several nights, he has tried to guess what the Golden Mountain is like. He's heard that the Americans there have hair of all different colors.

He guessed that they eat strange foods — maybe flowers or raw lava. And they are so tall they must have giant-sized furniture. Maybe they even sleep in tree branches.

The Golden Mountain has changed my brother. He's a whole different person now — one I like a lot better.

November 17

Blessing hangs around with the guest boys all the time now. He says he's going to the Golden Mountain as soon as Uncle sends for him.

Sometimes the guest boys can be snobs because they're so rich. However, Blessing is so popular that they welcome his company. I'm still the runt, though. When I tried to join them, they chased me away.

November 26

I don't believe all the stories the guest boys feed Blessing about the Golden Mountain. They say there are cards that can capture people's faces. And machines that eat mountains.

Blessing believes anything they say. He got mad at me when I told him his new friends were fooling him. He came close to hitting me like the old Blessing would have.

November 27

I was still puzzled about why Blessing got angry, so I asked Mother. She told me that sometimes dreams can be worse than opium or any drug. And it doesn't do any good to tell the dreamer to stop.

Then she found Blessing and told him there is no way any more of the family is going to that awful place.

Blessing was even more mad because I had told Mother his and Uncle's plan.

I don't understand my brother anymore. What kind of place can reach across a whole ocean and change someone that way? Only one that has powerful magic, I think. What will it do to Uncle? What will it do to the rest of us?

Tenth and Eleventh Months,
Year One of the Era, Prosperity for All

December 12

The days are short now. I feel as if Uncle took the sun away with him. If it isn't rain, then it's gloom, gloom, gloom.

Wars and rebellions have popped up all over the kingdom like weeds. That means even more taxes to pay for the new armies. I don't see why we give money to support a Manchu emperor we don't want in the first place. But we have no choice.

My parents sit up all night fretting. My mother jokes that we could pay the taxes if we gave up eating.

Poor Uncle. Poor us.

January 1, 1852

It's the American New Year. I wonder what they do to celebrate?

January 3

We had weed soup today. We can no longer afford to eat the rice we saved from our last crop. We'll have to use that for our taxes. So Mother gathered weeds from the fields and boiled them. They're bitter and horrible, but Mother said they would fool our bellies.

Mine didn't stay tricked for long, though. It started grumbling and growling the moment I set my bowl down.

January 4

Weed soup again!

January 5

Weeds. Ugh and double ugh!

January 6

Today Blessing found a boiled bug in his weed soup. I told him to be glad of the meat so he put it down my collar.

I was so mad. I thought my parents would be, too. They were too busy laughing, though. At least it took our minds off our troubles for a while.

January 11

My brother and I are growing thin. So are all the other boys in school. Piggy, though, is as round as ever. All the guest boys are. It's the magic of the Golden Mountain. It's a spell that protects them and their families.

Every night I say a prayer that Uncle will reach the Golden Mountain, too.

January 12

Mother asked my brother and me to help her find weeds. Almost everyone from the village was out hunting with us. Our valley has been picked clean.

The winter vegetable crops are rich. But they must all go to paying our rent and our taxes.

As I searched the dirt I could hear Piggy and the other guest children playing. And this evening they will sit down to their usual banquet of several courses. I know, because I can smell some of it cooking.

The magic of the Golden Mountain truly is powerful. But will its magic ever touch us?

◈ ◈ ◈

First Month,
Year Two of the Era, Prosperity for All

February 20
New Year's Day

Our Chinese New Year's was grim. Hardly any more weeds.
Father showed us a trick he used during the last famine. He
cuts off a young shoot from a tree and chews that.

February 27

All I can think of is food. Isn't that awful of me? I should
be worrying about Uncle.

March 8

Things get worse and worse.

My parents are talking about taking us out of school
and hiring us out. There is always lots of work for the
planting of the first rice crop.

Blessing looked happy, but I thought it was the worst
news of all.

Without my books, without school, I don't know what I'll do. With all due respect to Father, I don't want to work in the dirt all my life like some water buffalo.

March 18

I hold on to any hope. So when I saw the Crane passing through our village, I bolted from school and almost tackled him. My teacher shouted at me.

I knew he was mad and I would pay for it with bruises when I got back. However, I wanted to know if there was any word from Uncle.

Behind me I heard the other boys. At first I couldn't figure out why. Then I heard them talking about the odds, which are now fifteen to one. I guess they wanted to know if they had won their bet against Uncle. The vultures.

The Crane is a tall northerner who flew south and found a perch with a merchant in the city. As the merchant's clerk, he brings the remittances to the guest families along with any letters. Then he takes back any letters.

He recognized Piggy and the other guest boys, joking with them as he handed over the magical packets of money. Money that could let me stay with my books.

When I asked him about my uncle, the Crane looked down his long nose at me and said he didn't know a thing yet.

When will we get one of those magical packets?

I'd rather die than leave school.

I feel so ashamed. Uncle could be dead already. I have no right to write such things. But it is getting harder and harder to believe.

Please, Uncle. May you reach the Golden Mountain alive.

Second Month,
Year Two of the Era, Prosperity for All

March 23

Uncle arrived on the Golden Mountain!

You have to forgive me, my diary, if my writing is jiggly. I feel like dancing rather than writing. In fact, Blessing is still hopping around.

The Crane gave us a bundle full of cash. I've never seen so much in my life. There are strings and strings of coins. And that is just one month's remittance.

On top of the cash was a letter, but we're leaving that for later. There's too much happening at the moment. Mother says the letter will be the final treat for the evening.

I hope we don't sound heartless. We have kept our celebrating indoors with the door and shutters closed.

Poor Lucky and Virtue died during the voyage. The whole clan is stunned. They were sure the other two would make it rather than Uncle.

Lucky's parents were rich enough to buy his ticket overseas. However, Virtue had bought his ticket on credit. And now his family will have to make up the debt somehow. The Crane suggested that Virtue's wife sell her children.

We feel sorry for the others. If our hearts weren't singing, we would be wailing with them.

My parents are calling me. They want me to buy a fat hen from Piggy's family. (They have a big flock.) Tonight we're going to have a chicken. All of it!

I know just the one. Mmm!

Afternoon

As usual, Blessing disappeared when there was a chore to be done. I wound up plucking the chicken by myself.

What a mess! I had to save as many feathers as I could. Mother's hoping to stuff them into a cushion.

Early evening

What a feast!

Tomorrow Father's promised us pork. A prime cut, too. No gristle.

People have been coming by to congratulate Father. Some want him to invest in their schemes. Others need loans. Father and Mother promised Virtue's family that we will help them out. I am so proud of them.

Well, time to wash the dishes. Blessing's gone again. Guess who has to do it? But I don't care. Nothing can make me mad tonight.

Late evening

It's late, but Mother says I can burn the whole candle if I want to!

I like being rich.

Blessing showed up as soon as the last chores were done. Typical. He was collecting from Piggy on his bet.

Neither of my parents could read Uncle's letter, so they handed it to my brother. However, Blessing doesn't read very well. He handed it to me, saying that it was too dim inside the house for him. My eyes were better.

So I read Uncle's letter. After the standard good wishes, he said (I am copying from his letter), "The land of the Golden Mountain is everything I had hoped. We can get twice as rich if there are two guests here. Blessing is already fifteen and almost a man. Therefore, as head of the family, I command Blessing to join me."

Mother immediately began shouting that she wouldn't allow that. At the same time, Father was yelling that Uncle had lost his senses.

Meanwhile, Blessing leapt from the bench and began to

stamp his feet like a lion dancer. He began whooping that Uncle had remembered his promise. He halted only when Father ordered him to sit down. Blessing reminded Father that Uncle is the eldest. Father has to do what Uncle orders.

Right away Mother and Father retreated to their bedroom. They're still arguing.

Blessing and I should have shoved the table and benches to the side in the family room and spread out our sleeping mats. However, as soon as our parents were gone, Blessing began skipping around, saying that he is going to the Golden Mountain.

I've never felt happier and yet at the same time I've never felt sadder. On the one hand, Uncle made it to the Golden Mountain and found work. We are now a guest family.

But I am going to lose my brother. I'll miss him even more than Uncle when he leaves.

Hasn't he learned anything from our dead cousins? What if the voyage kills him?

I want to warn him, to beg him to stay. But what if my warning comes true? Sometimes to say something is to make it happen. And then I would feel awful.

Anyway, how can anyone say such gloomy things to someone who is so full of joy? It would be cruel to bring him down from his clouds.

Until now, my big brother has always protected me. Tonight I will protect him.

March 24

Blessing tried to get out of going to school this morning. He argued that a guest doesn't have to be smart, just lucky.

Mother used her broom to sweep him from the sleeping mat. She and Father still haven't decided if Blessing is going to be a guest.

My brother cheered up when he remembered all his winnings from the bet. I figured he would waste it all on candy and toys. However, he surprised me. He said he is going to keep it as his stake when he gets to the Golden Mountain.

At school, our teacher was ready with a half-dozen cards of carpenters and other businesses. We are now the family of a guest. So we have to start acting like one.

My rich cousins, the sons of guest families, also began to chat with us.

I can't get over the way the whole clan bows to us now. Before, we were one of the families that got snubbed at every turn.

If only we could enjoy Uncle's triumph. But Mother

and Father aren't speaking at home. Blessing is no help. He keeps reminding them that they have to do what Uncle commands.

Uncle's triumph has turned as sour as an unripe plum.

March 25

Mother and Father are arguing again tonight.

Blessing keeps insisting that they have to send him. I don't see how he can be so heartless.

Blessing says I'm jealous. I have to bite my tongue to say what I really think: that anyone with sense wouldn't want to go to that horrible place. With the exception of Uncle, of course.

I have only you, diary, to tell my worries to.

March 26

Father and Mother both look grim. I think they've decided to obey Uncle. But for some reason they haven't announced it yet.

Today Father took me down to one of our fields. I thought it was to tell me that Blessing was going to leave. However, Father just stood there and told me how much this earth means to our family. In fact, my great-great-grandfather died fighting a bandit on just this spot. So his blood is literally in the soil.

I didn't know why Father was going over family history that I already know. I waited patiently until he was finished. Then I told him that I understand that Blessing is leaving to help keep these fields. I promised him that I'll be right by his side doing everything I can to help him.

Father began to cry.

March 30

It's strange, but when Mother saw me this morning she broke into tears. I tried to ask her what was wrong, but she just shook her head.

April 1

Something is wrong. Blessing feels it just like I do. But we cannot figure out what. It is clear that he must go.

Maybe it's because the remittance won't cover the cost of his ticket. Perhaps they are upset that they have to sell the last field.

However, with two guests, we'll be getting twice as much money. We should be able to buy back the fields and get prime land as well.

April 7

I have not been able to write in here for several days because so much has happened. Mother and Father have come to a big decision:

I am to go. Not Blessing!

Blessing was mad because Uncle had wanted him and not me. Father insisted that if Uncle needed help, I would do just as well. That puzzled Blessing as much as it did me.

"But he's so small. What can he do?" Blessing protested. "I'm five years older and bigger and stronger. Runt's always got his nose buried in a book. How can he help Uncle carry the gold?"

Those were exactly my sentiments. I turned to Mother and asked her if she was really going to let me go.

Mother wouldn't look at me.

Blessing poked me and asked me if I wanted to leave.

Of course I don't. But I have to do what my parents say. So does Blessing. He's fighting a battle he can't win.

I thought writing in this diary would help, but I can hear Blessing arguing with our parents. He is saying they are condemning me to death.

I have to get out of the house.

Later

As soon as I stepped onto the street, cousins eagerly flocked over to me. All of them wanted some kind of favor.

I walked past them numbly. A dead person doesn't talk.

I kept telling myself that, but dead people don't feel hurt inside. Blessing is the strong one. He is the good-looking one. When we play games, he is always the first chosen. I am always the last. All our lives, he has been everyone's favorite.

Still, I hadn't thought my parents preferred him to me. Now I know better. They are willing to sacrifice me to save him.

My feet took me through the gates. The fields were waiting to be flooded so the rice seedlings could be transplanted from the tubs. When I got to Tiger Rock, I stared toward the Golden Mountain. The sun was starting to set over the hills, over the ocean, over the world that I am to cross. The world seemed so huge and I felt so tiny.

I am only thirteen, after all. Then I remembered what our teacher had said. Americans count your age only after you're born. By their standards, I am even younger — only twelve.

Maybe my luck is as small as Uncle's. Spinning on one foot, I chanted, "Spin around, turn around, luck changes."

Then I stroked the tiger's head.

I wonder if I'll ever see the sun set over these hills again.

Second Month,
Year Two of the Era, Prosperity for All

April 10
Somewhere in Southern China

I have not been able to make ink until now because I have been so busy traveling.

Two days ago Blessing walked with father and me as far as Tiger Rock. He still believes he should be the one leaving. I wish he were, too.

I was so scared, I was shaking a little. I tried hard not to, but I couldn't help it.

An odd thing happened then. Blessing stopped scowling and asked me why I always have my nose in a book. I thought it was a funny thing to ask at a time like this, but I told him I like going to faraway places and times.

Then he slapped me on the back and told me that I am getting what I want after all. It didn't make me feel any better. I appreciated his trying, though.

My legs felt as soft as bean curd when I stepped out of the valley with Father. I thought the sky was going to come crashing down and crush me.

Father and I didn't talk much on the way to the river-boat. I think he was too ashamed. I didn't know what to say either. What do you tell someone who wants to get rid of you?

On the riverboat I fell asleep. When I woke, my head was pillowed on his leg. He had slept sitting up, his head against the side of the boat.

How could he be so kind and yet send me away? His thoughtfulness only made me ache inside more.

April 11
Hong Kong

I don't know if I have enough pages to write about all the new things I've seen.

The city of Hong Kong is so much bigger than my village. So many tall buildings. And so many people! They seem to come from all over the province.

I saw my first British man, too. He didn't have horns like I expected. The British have done so many terrible things. About ten years ago, they invaded China and forced us to let them sell their drugs. They also made China give them land to build this city.

Besides his pale skin, the British man had hair the color of dirt and eyes like the sky. Other than his big nose, he looked human enough. Then I noticed the wiry curls on the backs of his hands, just like fur.

I clung to Father's coat until he found the address. It was a long, high-roofed warehouse. There was a desk right by the front door. Behind the desk was a clerk with a big, squat nose. He took one look at me and demanded my age.

When Father told him that I am just twelve, this man shook his head. He said I look a lot younger than twelve. If I were his son, he'd keep me at home until I put on a little more bone and meat. However, it was our business. He just sold the tickets.

Father and I looked at each other for a long time. Then he whispered, "Do your best. Watch over Uncle." And then he turned and disappeared into the crowd.

Impatiently, the man told me to follow him. When I didn't move fast enough, he grabbed my collar and dragged me past the desk and into an office.

Clerks were busy writing in ledgers. Others clacked the beads of abacuses and did calculations.

After taking down my name, the clerk told me that I will board ship in three days. Someone will call for me. After I get on the ship, Manchu and British inspectors will ask me some questions. It is to make sure I am going of my own choice. He said it all in a bored way, as if he had repeated the same speech thousands of times.

Then he asked me if I speak either English or Mandarin. I had to shake my head because all I know is my own local dialect. It was all right because an interpreter will be present to translate.

After some more paperwork, he asked if I could write my own name. I told him I could and signed it. Then he pointed me to a door and said to find a bunk. The huge room is filled with bunk beds, three beds high. They stretch as far away as I can see with enough men and boys to fill a village. I feel even more like a runt.

And my head buzzes with all the dialects.

I had to walk halfway through the building before I found a bunk. I'm surrounded by all these people and yet I've never felt more alone.

I've always been in Tiger Rock surrounded by the clan. Now I'm all by myself. When someone has a hand cut off, what does that hand think? Does it miss belonging to the body? That's how I feel. Like I've been cut off from something bigger. And now I've been tossed on the trash heap.

As soon as I found my bunk, I just had to write in my diary. I needed water to make ink, though. So I asked my neighbor where it was.

He had been sleeping with his hat over his face and his head on his small basket.

When he rolled on his side, I saw he was a man of about thirty years old. He had only one eye. A jagged scar ran across his left cheek. He pointed out where it was and then ordered me to leave him alone because he wasn't any nursemaid.

So I got the cup from my basket. When I started to leave, One-Eye stuck out his leg and told me to take my basket with me. I wasn't in bumpkin land anymore where people didn't know how to steal.

With my basket under my arm, I found the big jars of water. When I got back, I took out my inkwell and rubbed the ink stick in water.

I hear the dinner call. Time to line up. I don't want all the food to be gone by the time I get there.

Later

The meal was plain food like at home — vegetables and rice. But there was plenty of it.

Back to writing.

One-Eye is teasing me about being a scholar and keeps asking what I am doing with peasants like him.

But I keep my eyes on my diary. One-Eye scares me. I wonder if I'll live long enough to write in here again.

April 12

I never thought I'd see you again, dear diary.

This morning when I woke up, you were gone. So was the string of a hundred cash Mother had given me for luck money. That was more money than I'd ever had in my life. But I missed you the most.

I'd lost more than my notes. I'd lost my link to home. And I had lost my family again.

I was going to complain to the clerks. However, One-Eye just told me to save my breath. We are just so much meat to the clerks. They ship us here. They ship us there.

Though I did my best to wipe the tears away, One-Eye looked disgusted. Then he got out of bed and stomped away.

All I wanted to do was die. I curled up in a little ball and shut my eyes and wished that would happen. When I woke up, it was much darker in the warehouse. I must have slept for hours.

The next thing I knew, One-Eye was shaking my shoulder. There was a bruise on his cheek. He had my brush, my ink sticks, and my diary. But the money was gone. He said I should write it off as a fee for a lesson.

I asked him what lesson.

"Not to trust anyone," he told me. "Back in your village, the clan takes care of one another. Here it's every

41

man for himself. And it's cheap at the price. Some pay with their lives."

If I am upset over a little thing like this, he said, wait till I get to the land of the Golden Mountain. There are thieves there who would steal my teeth. I still have my shoes and clothes because I am so small. At night he takes the precaution of sleeping on his shoes, and he keeps his head on his basket. I should do the same from now on.

How could any place be worse than this?

In this huge building, I feel smaller than a runt, smaller than a bug. And I am only at the start of my trip to the Golden Mountain. What have my parents gotten me into?

When I tried to thank him, he warned me not to get the wrong idea. He had helped me because he didn't want me to cry all night. The noise might keep him up.

Only two things matter to One-Eye, his family and his clan. And that is it. He doesn't care a willow leaf about me.

He reminds me of a dog Uncle once had. The dog growled and barked a lot because he wanted you to stay away. If you were brave enough to get close, though, he would lick your face. I think One-Eye is that way. He likes to talk gruff and tough, but inside he is all soft.

As soon as I finish writing this, I will take One-Eye's

advice and store everything in my basket. Then I'll sleep with my head on top of it.

I just hope no one cuts my throat.

April 13

Obviously no one did.

I found out One-Eye's name. It's Sunny — which is the last name I'd pick for him. He comes from Two Streams village, which is four valleys over from Tiger Rock.

That makes us neighbors back at home. I am glad that my clan has not had any feuds with his. Otherwise we might be enemies.

I felt guilty over the things I had written about him. Nervously, I asked him if he had read my diary.

One-Eye said I couldn't possibly write anything of interest to him. And anyway, book learning is for cheats and scoundrels. An honest man does an honest day's work in the fields. He told me he doesn't have time for that nonsense.

I think it's his way of saying he can't read.

He asked me why I am keeping a diary anyway. So I explained about Uncle and my intentions to write the chronicle. I thought that was all he needed to know. I didn't think he'd understand how special you've become to me. He doesn't seem like the type.

April 14

I'm not a whiner. Even you, diary, must be getting tired of hearing me complain.

If I'm scared to be alone, I should do something about it. I'll find something or someone to belong to.

I'm going to try to find some more people from my district.

Later

Success!

I went through the aisles calling for anyone from our district.

A dozen others answered me. They're already as homesick as me. Though we don't come from the same village, there were some things we could talk about.

Of that dozen, three are also going on our boat. It has the American name of *Excalibur.*

My new friends' names are Gem, Squash-Nose, and Melon. They're feeling as alone and helpless as I am. We've decided to band together. We can watch one another's things and help one another in general. It'll be like our own little clan.

I invited Sunny to join our group. He told me I am living a fool's dream.

But I feel better. My group might be as ignorant as me, but I feel a little hope for the first time.

◈ ◈ ◈

Second to Fourth Months, Second Year of the Era, Prosperity for All

April 15
On Board the <u>Excalibur</u>

I was nervous during the inspections. I thought if I failed and they didn't let me get on the ship, I would stay in Hong Kong. I just couldn't face my clan.

However, they just repeated their questions impatiently. I answered their questions as the clerk had told me to do, and they let me leave. A hen at a poultry shop would have gotten more attention.

Our group had lined up together, so we went as a group into the dark hold of the ship. It is like a cave filled with bunk beds, but these are even narrower and smaller than the ones on shore. A grown man's nose almost brushes the bunk above.

Despite his words the other day, Sunny tagged along with us.

Men kept flowing past us to the other bunks. There were so many I thought the boat would sink. But my friends and I found berths together. To my surprise, Sunny wound up my neighbor. He claimed it was just chance. The last place he wanted to be was near a crybaby like me.

I think I know otherwise.

Later

When the parade of men finally stopped, I heard a rumble. A heavy grate had been put over the hold. The grate's bars made the hold seem like a prison.

Gem had heard a story. On another ship some pirates pretended to be coolies and got on board. When the ship set sail, they took it over and killed everyone.

But Sunny said the sailors are just afraid of us making a fuss.

When I asked him what kind of fuss, he told me I'd find out all too soon.

Melon asked him how he knows so much. It seems that Sunny has had three cousins who have made it overseas. Their letters have described the voyage.

April 25
Somewhere on the Pacific Ocean

Too seasick to write until today. Almost all of us have been ill.

It's also as hot as a stove inside the locked-up hold. And it's not even the warm season yet.

The smells only make me sicker. At first, some men who could move tried to go up on deck for relief, but the grate was locked.

So the healthier men sit on the stairs to get a draft of fresh air.

Once a day the sailors lower buckets to use for night soil. Then they haul up the used ones.

Sunny was the first to recover. He claimed his wife's cooking would toughen anyone's stomach. He brought us all bowls of rice in tea.

When I tried to thank him again, he growled at me in his usual way. He wasn't doing this because he liked any of us. He just didn't want us dying and stinking up the place any worse.

Melon was suffering the most from the seasickness. He was sure that if he died here, he was going straight to heaven after all this torture.

Sunny said there are worse ships. On those, one out of every three Chinese never reach the Golden Mountain. And there are better ships where everyone makes it.

I thought I knew what type of ship my uncle and cousins were on. But what kind of ship is this one? Maybe this will be my last entry. I wish I'd written better. My teacher would sniff at my penmanship and style.

May 4
Somewhere on the Pacific Ocean

I can barely write about this. I have never felt more humiliated. However, when I first began to keep you, diary, I decided I would tell you everything that happened. So that is what I must do.

At first I was glad when the sailors led a group of us up on deck. It was a little scary to be surrounded by that much water without any land in sight. But the fresh air felt good.

Then one of them said in broken Chinese that we had to take off our clothes. The sailors ripped the clothes off the ones who were slow. They wiped their hands afterward as if they had touched filth.

If they would let us out of the hold to wash, we wouldn't stink. I tried to tell them that. But they ignored me.

Then another group of sailors began bobbing up and down as they worked a pump. A third group picked up a hose and aimed it at us. I had barely taken a deep breath before the blast of cold salt water hit us.

The rest of the crew gathered around and made fun of us, pointing and laughing.

I'm not a human being to them.

I felt so angry. So did the others. Sunny was right. The

sailors don't keep us locked up because they're afraid we're pirates. They knew we would be angry at our treatment and are scared of us.

But if they treated us like humans, they wouldn't have to keep us in jail.

May 24
Somewhere on the Pacific Ocean

I have been too busy to write. Illness has swept through the hold. Every day we put corpses on the stairs and the sailors take them away. The bodies are dumped into the ocean. There will be no rest for their souls. You have to be buried in your home soil for that.

Strangely, except for the seasickness at first, I've felt well. So I've been trying to take care of our little group.

The others have recovered, but Sunny grows weaker and weaker. I don't know what to do for my friend. I feel so helpless I could cry. But tears would just make him mad. And so I hold them in.

May 29
Somewhere on the Pacific Ocean

Three more dead. Will any of us live?

June 3
Somewhere on the Pacific Ocean

Sunny asked me if I could write a letter. He was so embarrassed about it.

I was embarrassed, too. After all, I'm just a student. I've got no business writing letters as if I were a scholar. If I'd put on those airs back home, my teacher would have whacked me with his bamboo rod.

So I told him that as yet, I can write only regular Chinese. I don't know all the fancy classical words a real writer would know.

Sunny just said that his family wouldn't know it was him if it didn't sound plain.

I could see he really wanted me to, so I tore a page out and asked him what he wanted to say.

I have made a copy of his letter because I think it's what many of the men would have said.

> *Dear Wife,*
>
> *I know I promised that I would dictate a letter and tell you about the land of the Golden Mountain. But I don't think I'm going to get there.*
>
> *I can keep one small promise, though. With this letter you will receive the red silk ribbon for your hair. I bought it for you in the city.*

51

I'm sorry that I can't keep my other promises to you. I'll make it up to you in some other life. For as sure as I am there is a heaven, I am also sure we will meet again.

I will miss everything about home. I will miss waking every morning and listening to you start the fire in the stove. I will miss tickling our daughter and hearing her laugh. I will miss the sight of the wind rippling through the rice fields. I will miss walking with you up to the cemetery to visit our oldest boy.

There was more about what to do after he died. At first, I didn't want to put it down.

"You're not going to die, a tough man like you," I said.

"Here's a little bug like you scooting around, and a big man like me is laid low," he said. "Heaven must have a sense of humor."

"I'm doing this letter, but you can give it to your wife yourself when you go home. Then you can both have a good laugh," I said.

Sunny just smiled and went on.

At least Sunny owns three fields so his family could sell one of them to cover the debt.

When he was finished dictating, I signed his name and gave him the brush so he could make his mark.

He admired the letter. He hadn't known he had said so many words.

I apologized for my handwriting. I'd been only average for my class.

Sunny didn't care. He never thought he would see his thoughts down on paper like he was a scholar or an emperor or somebody important. He started to touch one of the words.

I warned him that the ink was still wet and might smudge. So he made a point of holding the letter by the edges as he gazed at it.

I have always enjoyed reading, but up until now I hadn't enjoyed writing. I got whacked too many times by my teacher for that. I was always writing the strokes of a word in the wrong order.

Now, though, I see that writing has its own power. It was like magic to Sunny.

Sunny said his oldest boy would have been my age if he'd lived. They had buried him right underneath a pine tree.

Then suddenly he looked shy. He had one more big favor to ask. Of course I said I'd do it if I could.

He wants to be mentioned in my book. He added quickly that it doesn't even have to be a whole sentence. Just his name.

Then he closed his eyes.

He only grunts when I try to encourage him. I wish I knew what to do. I've known him only a short while, but I feel like he's an uncle.

June 13
Somewhere on the Pacific Ocean

We put Sunny's body on the stairs. I feel like I will break inside. When will this trip ever end?

Even his ghost can't go home because his body is at the bottom of the ocean.

My tears are smudging the ink. Soon I won't be able to read this page. I have to stop.

June 17
Somewhere on the Pacific Ocean

We heard the thump of excited feet on the deck above. One of the sailors called down to us that we've made landfall.

Sunny almost reached the Golden Mountain.

I should be cheering like the others, but I have no laughter or smiles inside me.

Sunny is just another man who died trying to feed his

family. There will be no record of his family's grief when they get my letter. No one will know their tears.

But I will. And I will not forget.

June 18
San Francisco, or First City

The Golden Mountain is stranger, scarier, funnier, sadder and more wonderful than I ever imagined. Now that I am here I will use only the American calendar.

When we got off the ship, I thought I was in the middle of a forest. Except I could hear the ocean. Then I realized the tall poles were the masts of ships. I was surrounded by hundreds of empty boats. They jam the harbor like fish in my village pond. I bet I could have walked from one deck to another across the bay.

I didn't see any sailors. Instead, I saw laundry hanging from lines as if people were using the boats as houses. Then I saw one ship that literally had a house built on top of it. Maybe all the sailors had left their ships to find gold too.

Big, loud machines were pounding logs vertically into the mud a half-kilometer from shore. Real houses perched on top of logs that had already been driven in. Men and machines were filling in the shoreline to make more space.

In some places, they weren't even bothering to move the ship, but were just filling the dirt around it. Blessing would have loved the machines.

First City nestles at the foot of steep hills between the shore and the hillsides. A few houses lie scattered on the slopes. Instead of building on the hills, they're expanding into the water.

Though it's summer, the air is as chilly here as winter back at home.

I have to stop now. They're calling for us to register.

Later

Just got back. I don't want to forget a thing, so I'm going to write it all down. But there's so much.

After all these months at sea my legs are used to the motion of the waves. It was strange to stand on solid ground. My legs kept wanting to adjust for a moving platform. They still are.

On shore, there was a Chinese man shouting for people from the Four Districts to come over to him. Another was ordering Three Districts people to gather around him.

Gem, Melon, Squash-Nose, and I stuck together as a group. Our own district belongs to the area known as the Four Districts. We tried to ask the clerk what he wanted, but he looked impatient and bored. He snapped at us to wait and then went back to bawling out his call over and over.

When all the Chinese had left the ship, he mechanically began to recite a speech he must have given a hundred times.

It seems that the Chinese in the land of the Golden Mountain have grouped together by areas and family clans. But primarily by areas. His headquarters will act as our clearinghouse for everything — temporary shelter, jobs, and transportation to the gold fields. I was grateful to hear that.

The headquarters will also send our money and letters back home.

He emphasized that we will not be allowed to go home until we have paid back everything that we owe. If we die before then, they will see to it that our bones are shipped back for burial.

I felt a little trapped. It sounds as if the only way out of here is to die. But then I reminded myself that Uncle is doing well. He will watch over me.

Still later

Finally, real food! Rice, vegetables, and meat! At first, I wondered if I had lost track of time. Maybe it was a feast day. However, the people at the headquarters act like they have it all the time. At home only rich people can feast like this every day.

To get to Chinatown we had to pass through the American part of the city. San Francisco is like a big pot of stew with everything mixed in.

People seem to live in anything they can. In many places, I saw tents of dirty canvas. Other buildings were wooden fronts with canvas sides and roofs that flapped up and down. The first good wind ought to blow most of them away. When I asked the clerk, he explained that in the past three years, six fires had destroyed the city. The latest was just a year ago.

Then I saw some little cottages built out of iron. The clerk said that there used to be a lot more. However, in the last fire, many people had stayed inside them, thinking they were safe. Unfortunately, the flames turned the iron cottages into huge stoves. When the unlucky people tried to escape, they found the doors and windows had sealed tight and they were trapped. Most of them died.

Finally, we came to an area that the fire must have skipped. Tall buildings of brick or wood rose several stories high. Through the open windows and doorways came the sound of loud laughter. Gem tried to peek inside one place and got a hard-boiled egg in the face. He said they were gambling and drinking inside.

Other wooden buildings were so new that their lumber smelled of freshly planed wood and shone like pale gold. Still others had already weathered gray while a few had been painted white, the color of death. At first I thought they were mausoleums for the dead. But as I passed I saw they were stores. All of them were crammed with goods. In fact, the goods spilled out of some them and were piled on the sidewalk.

Then I saw tall stone walls rising from the dirt. Chinese were on scaffolding building the walls, so I thought we were in Chinatown. However, when we just kept on walking, I asked the clerk.

He said it is an American building, but that tall mountains shut off this province from the rest of the country. It had been cheaper to bring the stones from China. Unfortunately, the assembly instructions had been written in Chinese, so the American owner had hired a boatload of Chinese stone masons to put it together. It is to be the First City's first building of stone. I feel proud that it is Chinese who are doing that.

Have to go. Gem and Melon need help reading the employment notices.

Evening

San Francisco is also a big stew of people. Every country in the world has dumped someone into the pot. And most of us are hurrying to the Golden Mountain.

I've seen hair of almost every color, and faces and bodies stranger than the British man in Hong Kong. Many of them are Americans, but many others speak languages that don't sound like English. They wear every type of costume from elegant to cheap and plain.

I also see people with skin the same color as mine. However, when I try to greet them, they don't understand me. I don't think they are speaking English, either.

Most of them are miners and look as eager and new as us.

The air is crackling with energy. I wish I could bottle it and sell it as a tonic.

Two things worry me, though. Even if the Golden Mountain is pure gold, can there really be enough for all the miners I see?

Almost all of them are armed with at least a pistol and a knife, too. Why do they need so much protection? And from what?

Could the Golden Mountain be even more dangerous than the sea voyage here? I don't see how. And yet. . . .

The others want to turn off the light so they can sleep.

Another wonder. The light is inside glass. The Americans call it kerosene.

I don't see how they can sleep. I know I won't.

June 19

Another big meal. It was rice porridge and fried crullers like at home. But the porridge had big chunks of pork and preserved eggs. I've never eaten so well. Blessing would definitely have liked this part of the trip.

The Chinese live in an area on a steep hill of San Francisco. The clerk was careful to tell us the Chinese and American names in case we get lost. In Chinese, it's the street of the people of T'ang. The T'ang was a famous dynasty back in China a thousand years ago. In English, it is called Sacramento Street.

However, since there are thousands of Chinese living here now, Chinatown has begun to spill over onto other streets, especially Dupont.

Like the American town, Chinatown is a mixture of wooden buildings and tents. The buildings are American-style but wooden carvings and signboards in Chinese mark their owners.

Above Chinatown, on an American street called Stockton, are a few wooden mansions where the richer Americans live.

Our group is luckier than some of the Chinese who have to stay in tents. We're inside the headquarters itself. The smells make me feel right at home. Altar incense mixes with the smell of cooking.

We are crowded into a room on the second floor. Though we are packed side to side, it seems spacious after the *Excalibur*.

Later

Sad news. My three friends have decided to head for the southern mines. I tried to talk them into going to the northern ones where Uncle is. He's at some place called Big Bend. But the clerk said the weather will be better in the South.

I will be alone again.

When it was my own turn with the clerk I had a bad scare. Naturally, Uncle had put my brother's name on the forms and not mine.

That seemed to exasperate the clerk. (He was the same bored man who met us on the wharf and guided us here.)

At first, I was afraid I was going to be sent back. But somehow I straightened things out. When my business was done, I held out Sunny's letter and asked him to send it to Two Streams. The clerk seized my hand instead. I got ready to punch him, but then he demanded to know how I'd gotten ink stains on my fingers. I told him I had been writing in my diary last night. It isn't always easy to wash off the ink.

The clerk looked doubtful and insisted I take some dictation.

My parents have taught me not to show off. However, that stung my pride. So I took the brush. When I dipped the brush into the ink, it gave off this wonderful perfume. I could still see part of the picture of the carp on the side of the ink stick. It looked like ink a rich, important scholar would use.

Of course when I hesitated, the clerk thought that proved I was lying and couldn't write. That made me nervous again and I told him I was just admiring the ink.

He took on a smug look then. In Chinatown, he got only the best. He was glad to see that I could appreciate it.

I noticed that the paper was good quality too. So was the brush.

When I asked him what he wanted me to write, he dictated a simple letter with basic words. It was easier than my teacher's tests at home, which had hard, complicated words from the classics.

The clerk beamed when he looked at the dictation. I don't know why. My writing is clear and legible but hardly elegant. My teacher always shook his head when he graded my handwriting.

Still later

The clerk came by to offer me a job!

So many Chinese come in every day that headquarters is buried in paperwork. That's the literal truth. His little office was crammed with stacks of papers.

For a moment I was tempted. To live in the First City and see all of its wonders every day. To make my living by writing and reading. That all sounded like paradise.

Then I remembered my uncle. So I refused politely. But the clerk wouldn't give up. He offered to write a letter. He said that if my uncle had any kindness in him, he would let me stay here.

I told him, though, that my uncle had sent for me to help him pick up the gold nuggets — the ones as big as melons.

He just sighed. When I learned my lesson — and if I survived — there would be a job waiting for me, he said.

I have this funny feeling in my stomach again. I have to admit it's a bit odd. Why would anyone sit cooped up in a tiny office if there are such big nuggets to be scooped up? Maybe it won't be as easy as Uncle told me.

When he left, I went down to the little altar in the headquarters. There were some incense sticks in a cup. I took out one of them and lit it from a candle. Then I set it in a cup of sand and said a prayer for Sunny.

I burned some incense for me, too.

June 20
Somewhere northeast of San Francisco

This morning I boarded a smaller boat by myself. It traveled across a broad bay and then through a series of smaller ones to a river.

The boat is crammed with miners traveling to the gold country. They clump together in groups, each of which talks a different language.

Because I couldn't find water, I couldn't write, so I got bored. There were some other Chinese on board, but they were busy gambling. They wouldn't have allowed me to join even if I had had money.

So I wound up drifting over to the side of the boat to look at the water. Suddenly, a fish leapt out of the water. Its sides shone in the sun so it looked like a silver arrow. It was so lovely it would be a shame to eat it.

When the fish splashed back into the water, I felt a nudge in my side.

I spun around to defend myself. I saw an American boy with hair the color of fire. He looked to be about the age of Blessing. He grinned and pantomimed fishing.

I guess he had been thinking some of the same things.

Through signs, we learned each other's names. It took a while to work out his name because his name was in reverse. In China, your family name is the most important thing, so we put our family's name first and our personal name second. Americans must think the opposite, because they put their personal names first and their family names last. Strange. His personal name is Brian. His family name is Mulhern.

He's just as curious about me as I am about him. After a while, I forgot about how strange he looked.

Unfortunately signs got us only so far. So then he took out what I thought was a stick. It ended in a point with some black stuff. He called it a pencil.

He was able to write on the deck without a brush and ink. I don't think I will ever give those up since the writing is nicer to look at, but the pencil is handier when you're traveling.

Then, through pictures and signs, I learned that he is not an American. He comes from a country called Australia. I'm embarrassed to say that I have never heard of it. If I understand him right, his country is to the south of China.

I wish we had studied more about the world. However, our teacher felt that China was the most civilized country in the world. Why should we study any other place? We had learned about the Golden Mountain only because our clansmen were going there.

I admired his pencil so much that he gave it to me. I tried not to take it but he insisted. My new friend has a big heart.

I am writing this with my new writing implement. No more ink sticks. No more inkwells. No more finding water.

Later

I've already worn down the pencil. Brian showed me how to whittle the pencil with a knife to keep the point. I used it to draw him a crude picture of home, which I gave him as a present.

A boy with skin as dark as mine came over. Over his clothes he wore what looked like a black woolen blanket with a hole cut through the center for his head. Bright yellow, red, and blue stripes decorated the bottom.

Like Brian, he puts his family name last, but his personal name is Esteban and through our system we learned he is from Chile. Then a fourth boy joined us. He has hair the color of mud. His name is Hiram and he is a real

American. Hiram and Brian speak different dialects of the same language. Hiram is a year older than Brian. Esteban is about a year younger.

A fifth boy is Jubal. His skin is even darker than mine. He is as old as Hiram and is the slave to a tall golden-haired man.

In the hundred men and boys on the deck, at least ten countries are represented. Maybe even more.

It's now a game of signs and pictures as we try to communicate.

We come from all parts of the world. Brian and I traveled east. Esteban came north. Hiram came west from the other coast of America, which he referred to as the *States*.

That puzzled me a bit. Most of the states are in the eastern half of America beyond the mountains. But according to Hiram, California is also a state.

California was taken from the southern country of Mexico only four years ago. Normally, a territory would have to wait years before being promoted to a state. However, as soon as gold was discovered here, America didn't want to lose California and made it a province right away.

Jubal and his owner came across the land with a large group from the province called Missouri. Of their group of ten, they lost three.

Hiram has an older cousin who traveled here three

years ago, sailing all the way around the continent of South America. Hiram and his older brother set out by boat to join their cousin, but because their cousin had encountered fierce storms at the southern tip of South America, they traveled south only as far as a place called Panama.

There, they got off one boat and walked across the Panama isthmus instead. On the other side they boarded a boat to go north to San Francisco. However, his brother got sick and died on the boat.

It is dangerous no matter how you try to reach the Golden Mountain. I look around the crowded boat. For every person here, I wonder, how many more died on the way?

We have begun to teach one another words in our languages. Mostly we try to ask Hiram questions about America. There is so much we need to know about our new home.

Hiram has been very patient. He's curious about us, too. He wants to know why we're going to the gold fields. (That's what the Americans call the Golden Mountain. Or sometimes Hiram calls it the gold country.)

Brian laughed and said he is here to get rich. Hiram wants enough money to buy his own farm some day. He wants to marry a girl back home.

I didn't know enough American to explain all the reasons why I'm here. It isn't just a question of becoming rich or buying land.

Brian nodded and said in the end we aren't here for the money or for the land or for our families. We are all dreamers. And not just ordinary dreamers. There are plenty of folks at home who talk about their dreams and do nothing. However, each of us here have risked our lives to make our dreams come true.

I bet everyone on board the boat has done the same thing. Maybe almost everyone I met in San Francisco.

We all sat for a moment thinking about that. We have gotten past so many dangers already. Surely we'll survive the new ones.

Hiram is the most unselfish fellow. When we have all found our dreams, his house and his farm will be open to all of us, too.

Still later

A group of white men just came over to us. I couldn't understand why they were so mad at Hiram.

The words flew by too fast for me to follow. But Brian explained that the men are Americans. They didn't like Hiram being friendly to us. In fact, they don't like foreigners at all. They want all foreigners to go home. That means not only Esteban and myself but Brian, too.

I couldn't understand what they were saying, but their faces were ugly masks.

Some men in Brian's and Esteban's groups started to shout back. I looked around. All the men had guns and knives. I was afraid there was going to be a battle right there on deck.

However, bullies are alike all over the world. The first group retreated.

I felt scared then. I am so far from China. Esteban was just as upset. Even Brian looked afraid. Then Hiram hugged each of us in turn.

As long as there are enough Americans like him, I won't worry.

June 22
Sacramento, or Second City

I might as well bring this up to date while I'm waiting in line.

I made it to my next stop. It's SO hot here. Just like at home in Tiger Rock. About now we'd be holding the Dragon Boat festival. Crews would paddle dragon-shaped boats in races. The air would be so damp my clothes would stick to me. The air is drier here.

Once we got off the boat in Sacramento, I had to find the Chinatown. Luckily, Brian and Hiram had taught me a little about their simplified system of writing. English is so strange. Instead of thousands and thousands of characters to learn, they have only twenty-six characters, which they call the alphabet. These characters combine to make words. But they write everything backward, from left to right in horizontal lines. Chinese write from right to left in columns.

After having to memorize Chinese characters, it was easy to learn their twenty-six. (Of course, putting the pictures together into words is another matter, but I am determined to learn.)

In Chinatown I found the local headquarters of the Four Districts where there are lines of Chinese waiting to check in. It's my turn. Have to go.

Later

I hate paperwork. There's always so much of it. When I was finally finished, the clerk tried to steer me into the store to buy outfits. He said that I'll need a warm coat and boots. Even in the summer, it is cold up in the gold country. And in the winter, there is snow.

So I looked, but all the prices were in American dollars. When I asked what the exchange rate was, I was shocked. I had thought my stolen string of a hundred cash was a fortune, but not here. All the strings of cash — the wealth Uncle had sent home — was worth only a few American dollars here. So I said they cost too much. The clerk said I'll be sorry.

I joined a group of miners on their way to the gold country. Hiram is here, too. He looks just as glad to see me as I am him. It turns out we're both heading to Big Bend.

The whole party numbers about thirty, and I am the only Chinese.

Hiram and I try to talk to others, but it is hard work. We have so few words in common. However, we figured out that the men in our party come from twelve countries! Many of the lands are ones I've never heard of.

June 23
In the Gold Country

Hiram and I are both the curious types. We've found a driver who lets us sit with him on the wagon seat.

There is no Golden Mountain! The gold is scattered all around the mountains instead. Some of it is in the ground. Some of it washes down the rivers.

I feel so dumb. The Golden Mountain is a fancy, poetical name. It's not the literal truth.

June 26

The mountains rise steadily before us. We are following a trail eastward along a wide, quiet river.

The driver explained that the river is swollen from the winter snow melting in the mountains.

Snow.

I've read about it but I've never seen it. Snow never fell in Tiger Rock, only in northern China where it was cold in the winter.

I hope the snow lasts long enough for me to touch it.

June 27

The land has begun to rise, forming rolling foothills. It is dry here. The grass covering the hills has already dried up to a dull gold. The trees are scarcer and different. They grow in hollows between the hills where they can get water.

June 28

The going is getting harder. The road is sandier and the wagon often gets stuck. We all pitch in to help get it out.

Beside us, the river is narrower and deeper now. Its

waters foam along the rocks like white scales on a dragon. When I was thirsty, I put my hand in for a drink. The water is as cold as ice. My fingers feel numb. The driver wasn't joking when he said it was melted snow.

June 29

Great slabs of rock thrust up from the dirt. Somehow scraggly bushes and trees cling to the ledges. The air has begun to grow colder.

I wonder if the clerk was right about the clothes and boots?

Later

We passed by a bearded man kneeling on the riverbank. The driver told Hiram to remember what the man looked like. His kind are disappearing. At first, I thought his clan was losing a feud with another clan and I asked about that through Hiram.

The driver just laughed and explained that three years ago at the start of the gold rush, you could find gold by just dipping a pan into the river. Prospectors like him once covered the riverbank like ants, panning for gold.

Sure enough, he had a pan in his hands, which he

dipped into the swift water. Then he took it out, swirled the water out, and sifted through the mud and pebbles for bits of gold or even dust. And now that I know how cold that water is, I don't see how he could do it.

I stared hard at the water for the glint of gold. To be honest, I had expected to see some nuggets by now. However, all I saw was rocks.

The driver says the bearded prospector is a fool. The area here was used up long ago.

I couldn't hold it anymore and asked through Hiram where the melon-sized nuggets are. The driver laughed even louder and said there never were any. If there were, he'd be back in Boston instead of driving a wagon.

I feel like an even bigger fool. Why did I listen to Uncle's fantasies?

June 30

I guess the driver was right when he said the area is played out. We pass by empty cabin after empty cabin. Tall weeds grow in the doorways. They must have been abandoned for a year or more.

We have been traveling up a path that angles more than forty-five degrees. It is so steep that the heavily loaded pack mules have often balked.

We travel now between giant sheets of rock bigger

than houses. The only sign of life is us. Everyone has grown quiet.

Though it is hot in the day, it is freezing at night. I wish now that I could have bought that coat and boots in Sacramento. I sit and shiver at night.

July 1

I've met the hungriest Americans I have ever seen. They were so thin their limbs were like sticks. Their faces were all bony, too. And they were the first Americans I saw in rags.

They gathered around the wagons and begged for supplies. They recently came from the other coast like Hiram. However, they had walked west, instead of taking a boat.

I hadn't realized how big America is. Hiram explained that the men had crossed wide plains and high mountain ridges. Several of their party died along the way. The survivors looked like they're one step from the grave themselves.

The drivers gave them what they could.

I thought of all the dangers the miners had risked and all the hardships they had gone through.

Was the gold worth it? Were our dreams?

There was something familiar about the newcomers.

As I stared at their gaunt faces, I realized what it was: their faces were the faces of starvation.

Back in China, those had been our faces. The cheekbones of my parents' faces had stood out just like theirs. I never want to see that again.

The dream is the right one. As scared as I am, I have to try to find gold.

July 3

I've seen my first real claim! Five Americans work together. A ditch directs water into a long wooden trough some five meters long. The driver called it a *long tom*.

Gold is heavier than mud and rocks. So dirt by the shoveful is dropped at the top of the trough. The trench is set at an angle so the water carries the mud and rocks away. Wooden cleats have been nailed to the bottom to catch the gold.

Then they take the gold inside their cabin and dry it at night by the fire.

Since it is hard to get gold, most of the prospectors have banded together. But the driver says even that way of working is doomed.

July 4

The Americans are celebrating the birthday of their country. They are shooting off guns since they don't have firecrackers.

July 5

I've finally seen a gold mine.

When I first felt the ground shaking, I thought it was an earthquake. The driver said it was caused by a quartz mill.

Since the gold is gone from the river, the Americans have turned to the land where gold can be found in white rock called quartz.

Our trail ran above the operation, so I could see how it works. There is a huge hoist over a vertical shaft. Pumps keep the water from flooding it.

Carts then take the raw ore to a stamping mill, which crushes the quartz. The gold is separated from the fragments. The mill makes a frightful noise.

It takes a lot of men to build and operate the quartz mills, and they are having a hard time finding gold. The driver says they are no longer individuals with a dream, just employees hired to do a job.

July 7

Our party has begun to split up into smaller groups that head up trails to their companies. The wagon is much lighter and the mule train is much shorter, too, as we drop off supplies. However, the road is even steeper, so we do not move any faster.

July 11

The guest boys weren't fooling us after all. The Americans really do have a machine that eats mountains. I'll have to tell Blessing when I write to my family.

It's really a system of machines and troughs that guide the water into a single hose.

The water from the hose washes the gold out of the dirt, where more machines collect it. But the flow chews at the mountain like the snout of a huge monster.

The driver says that since gold is getting harder and harder to find, these monster machines will be the only way. There won't be people anymore. Just gears in a machine.

The driver says this is the future for all miners.

I'm getting scared again. Maybe Father was right: it would be just Uncle's luck to come to a place after all the easy gold is gone.

July 12
Big Bend

Finally, Big Bend!

It's at a spot where the river curls around in a tight loop. The land all around here is pockmarked with little holes. Here and there, a few hard-bitten miners pop up and down like small animals.

The town itself sits on top of the hill. It's all tents of dirty canvas — like sooty turtles squatting in the dirt. The driver has stopped by a tent with a signboard in American. It seems to be a store. He is dropping some things off there, and then still has a few more stops to make before leaving.

I feel sad. Hiram and I have to separate here. However, we have promised to see each other when we can.

Later

I found Uncle!

The driver told me to follow a path. It went on for a kilometer to a curving branch of the river about ten meters wide. It was lined with all kinds of trees. There I found about fifty Chinese cutting down trees.

Uncle was among the men using American axes and long, two-person saws. I guess I had been picturing him as a rich, wealthy man directing his workers. But Uncle looked dirtier and more tired than he had ever been at home.

I didn't see any gold nuggets around — bean-sized or melon-sized. It's what I was afraid of. The gold is just as scarce here as down below.

Uncle dropped his ax when I called to him. "What are you doing here? I sent for Blessing."

What he meant was, he wanted someone big like Blessing, not a runt like me. I didn't know how to tell him that my parents had wanted to risk only me and not my brother. All I could do was apologize for disobeying him.

Uncle said he'll get me back to China somehow, even if he has to borrow the money.

I'm going to get a small ax and start trimming the branches off a tree. I might not have Blessing's size, but I've got twice the determination.

Twilight

Uncle has had to admit that though I'm small, I can work. I guess I got my muscles from doing Blessing's chores as well as my own.

Uncle's boss is a man from Red Hill back at home. Uncle calls him the Fox, but he doesn't look like one.

He's bald with sleepy eyes. He looks like he ought to be peddling vegetables.

He doesn't think much of me, either. He says I am too small to be of much help.

Uncle explained that there had been a mix-up. He had asked for my older brother.

I felt so ashamed — as if we had played a nasty trick on Uncle. So I just started to trim the tree again. After watching me, the Fox had to admit that I could hold my own. He offered me seventy-five cents a day. It's not much, but I can't be picky.

We didn't stop until sunset, so it made for a long day. However, I'm used to working that long at home during harvest and planting time.

I'd never felt more sore or tired. American soil looks like Chinese soil, but it seems to grow heavier and heavier with every shovelful.

By the time we went to wash up, we were covered with dirt. Uncle laughed when we saw his reflection. He said he had come here to get away from the dirt and now look at him.

Have to stop now. Time to eat.

Early evening

I'm stuffed! All the vegetables and meat are salted or pickled, but there's lots of it.

Basically the cook boils a big wok of rice and then puts pickled vegetables and salted fish and sausages on top. The steam from the rice cooks the sausages and fish at the same time. A kettle of tea heats next to the pot.

It is more food than I'd ever had at home, and Uncle said that we will have meat every Sunday, usually a chicken but sometimes a pig or even beef.

During supper, I brought Uncle up to date on our family and what his money had already done for us.

And now we can send home double. Uncle is full of plans.

I just caught a fellow staring at me. I think his name's Prosperity. I wonder what he wants? He looks harmless, but I'll watch out for him.

Uncle wants to show me our mining operation, so I'll finish when I get back.

Late evening

We went over to the river. I could hear the roar from the rapids about five hundred meters above. Here the river widened and the water slowed. Uncle said it was a natural spot for the gold to drop out of the water.

He explained that we are going to construct what the Americans call a wing dam. We will build a wall from the riverbank out into the river. Then we will build another wall at right angles to the first, cutting off an area of the riverbed. From that we will pluck our gold.

I dipped my hand into the water. It was icy cold. More melt-off from the snow on the mountaintops.

As I rubbed my numb hand, I wondered how we are ever going to get the gold out of its freezing clutches. I asked if we would find melon-sized nuggets. Uncle shook his head sadly. The gold will be dust.

So the driver was right. Uncle had just been talking big again. I just hope there is some gold left.

July 13

For breakfast we had rice porridge with sausages and crullers. I've never eaten so well in the morning.

It helped make up for last night. Though the day was hot yesterday, the night was so cold that I didn't sleep too well.

Like a lot of men here, Uncle has gotten American clothes. They were made for this climate. My own thin cotton clothes are meant for the tropics at Tiger Rock. That clerk in Sacramento was right. I do need boots and a coat. I shiver and cough most of the time.

Time to go to work. Tree trimming should warm me up.

Afternoon

Really hot this afternoon. The sun beat down on me like a hammer. And I swallowed as much dirt as I shoveled. A lot of it stuck to my throat. All I could think of was how nice it would be to work in the cool water.

Then I remembered how cold that water really is, and I was glad I was on the land.

All I do now is trim trees and haul away the branches. I'm no better than water buffalo plowing a field.

It's been so long since I've read a book. And I'm so tired from work that it's hard even to think. I almost didn't write today. But I can't let that happen. One day would lead to two, and then a week. And then I'd stop completely.

And then maybe my mind would go dead, too. Then I really wouldn't be any better than a buffalo.

I wonder if Hiram is just as tired as me. The Americans are building a big dam across the river itself. So he's probably just as busy.

Am I sounding like I'm whining? I shouldn't. The work gives me the money to help my family. And there's Uncle to watch over.

That Prosperity fellow is always bragging. Most everyone tries to avoid him. So far he hasn't said anything to me, but I catch him staring. Like now. I still can't figure out what he wants.

Time to eat. Dinner smells good.

July 14

Cold last night. Hot today. I heard an animal howling. Uncle says it was a coyote.

I finally found out what Prosperity wants. As I was starting to write today's entry, he asked me to write a letter to his family back in China.

I told him what I had told Sunny — that I am no scholar. But his face reminded me of my dead friend. It's kind of hungry. Not for food but for home.

So I tore a page from my diary. For a letter home, I thought I should get out my brush and inks and inkwell. Prosperity watched, fascinated as I filled the well with a little water and then rubbed the ink stick against the side until the ink was just right.

The letter itself took only a little longer than mixing

the ink. Prosperity apologized to his family for not sending home as much this month but promised five times as much next month. He has some business investments that are going to pay off soon.

When I had signed his name and let him make his mark, I was surprised when he left an American coin. It was a copper one called a penny.

I told him that the letter was free. He wouldn't take the coin back, though.

Uncle had been on my other side. He was curious about Prosperity's investments, but Prosperity only apologized. He couldn't tell anyone or they might want in on it, too.

Uncle looked so sad that I asked him what was wrong. He said he is letting our family down because he isn't as successful as Prosperity.

Before I could try to comfort him, another man came over and also wanted a letter written.

And then there was a third. Word must have spread through the camp. Even the cook came to have a letter written.

By the time I was finished, Uncle was already asleep. So it's too late to talk to him. I'm starting to yawn myself.

July 15

I've been doing letters for all the others. Though I'm still just as tired from work, it's nice to feel needed. I may not be able to shovel or haul as much dirt as they can, but I can do something most of them can't.

And I've got a small pile of pennies now. At first, I thought of saving up for a coat and boots. However, Uncle's still been moping around. He has not been the same since he heard Prosperity boasting.

I know. I'll give my pennies to him. We'll tell our family that one of Uncle's investments is paying off. And in a way, it is. After all, he brought me over here.

It's not a lot, but I'll feel like I'm helping out.

I'm worried about paper. At the rate I'm writing letters, I will run out of it soon.

I'm going to the Fox's tent. Most people stay away from there because he doesn't like to be bothered after work. I'm going to ask him to have blank notebooks brought up with the next batch of supplies. After all, I can pay for them now.

Later

When I poked my head inside the Fox's tent, he said he'd seen me writing letters. Can I cipher as well and use an abacus?

I told him I can do that a little.

He held up a hand that is so covered with calluses, it is as leathery as a horse's hide. He told me his fingers were meant more for holding a shovel than a brush. If I could help him keep the accounts he would pay me a full salary and keep me in all the paper and ink I needed.

I thought of the clerk's fancy ink sticks and fine writing paper and asked for good ones.

The Fox must be desperate, because he agreed.

I thought I'd just cut down trees in America. However, maybe America needs strong minds as much as it needs strong backs.

Perhaps there is a place for me here after all.

Evening

It's late now. I've been learning the Fox's bookkeeping system. But I also want to write down all the secrets I picked up.

Uncle sent so much money home, I thought he must

be earning a fortune here. However, he's making only two dollars a day! Sixty dollars a month isn't a lot — especially when he has to pay for his own food and other items.

American dollars must be worth more in China. And the pennies I earn for letter writing will be useful after all.

The other thing is that Uncle is listed as a skilled carpenter. That was news to me. The most he'd done in China was make shelves and little boxes.

I had another surprise when I saw how much the others like Prosperity are getting. They are getting only a dollar and a half, and the Fox added on expenses for food and other items.

Uncle and I are the only ones who bought our own tickets. The others are still paying off theirs. The Fox deducts a certain amount each month and sends it to San Francisco to be passed on to the various people who own the notes.

As I went over the entries in the ledger, I realized that not only does Prosperity owe someone for his ticket, but he has also borrowed heavily from the Fox. He has a whole page of debts that will take him fifteen years to pay off.

The Fox made me promise not to tell anyone. He explained that Prosperity kept coming to him with sob stories about home. He believed them until he learned that Prosperity was gambling it all away. There won't be any more loans. So much for Prosperity's business investments.

The Fox had a letter for Uncle. It was in a pile of mail that came today. I can't wait to read it. I even sniffed it to see if I could smell something from home. Too many hands had handled it, though.

When I got back, to my disappointment, Uncle wasn't in the tent. The others said he went out for a walk. Probably to mope.

I was tempted to open the letter myself. I started writing in my diary to distract myself.

I hear Uncle's footsteps now.

Later

Uncle was just as excited about the letter as I was. His hands shook as he opened it. Father had Blessing write it. I'm copying some of it:

> How are you? It has been terrible here in China. It has not stopped raining since Runt left. The floods have ruined the first rice crop. Prices are already rising on everything. Heaven knows what we will do if we lose the next.

There was more bad news about the wars and rebellions. Yet another group of Chinese was trying to overthrow the Manchus. They had won a big battle. Normally, I would have cheered, but now there were more taxes to pay for a new Manchu army.

So we thank heaven for the money you send to us. In other villages that are guestless, families have had to sell everything, even themselves. We have prospered. And our clan survives, thanks to you. I hope you don't mind. We have had to postpone plans to buy more fields because we are helping out the clan. Could you send more money?

Everyone blesses your name, Precious Stone.

Then the letter went into gossip about the clan that I don't think has any place in a serious book like mine.

Blessing added at the bottom:

Our teacher gives us more and more homework. You don't know how lucky you are.

Blessing doesn't know what luck is. I would trade places with him in the blink of an eye.

Uncle had been awfully quiet. I caught him with his

legs crossed, studying one of his boots. He said he had been going to get a new pair, but he supposed he could patch them instead. Then we could send more money home.

I thought of the baby chicks demanding to be fed. It doesn't seem fair. They don't know how little we actually get.

Uncle, though, liked the fact that the clan blessed his name. Before, he was a joke.

I decided to beg some candles from the cook. That way I can write more letters. If I send more money, maybe the clan won't think of me as Runt anymore.

July 16
Big Bend

I'm scared.

At first, I didn't pay any attention to the American when he walked into camp. However, all around me the other miners jerked their heads around like a flock of startled birds.

Uncle got hold of me and told me to be careful because the tax man was here.

Uncle explained that the Americans tax foreign miners. They had started it last year. The price was very high at twenty dollars a month. The purpose was to drive a lot of the Australians and the South Americans from the gold fields. And it had. So they had stopped the tax.

But recently, the Americans had passed another law. This time mainly against the Chinese.

The other miners reluctantly began to pull out their money. For three dollars they received a slip of paper. That was their license for the month. They would need that to be able to work in the gold fields.

At least the tax is lower, but three dollars a month is still a lot of money. It means a lot of food or clothes that couldn't be bought at home.

Uncle paid the tax man for both him and me and got our "licenses" for the month.

Suddenly the tax man shouted something. I saw Prosperity trying to slip into the trees. Prosperity started to run then, and the tax man pulled out a gun and shot him. With a scream, Prosperity went down. He was holding his leg, so I guess he had been hit there. Prosperity tried to make excuses, but the tax man didn't understand his Chinese.

Everyone else was just standing around. "We've got to stop him," I said to Uncle. Uncle held me tight. The tax man could do anything he wanted to collect the taxes.

I turned to the Fox and begged him to lend Prosperity the money. The boss refused, saying that he had already told me why he couldn't.

"But when his business investments come in, he'll pay you," Uncle said.

It was on the tip of my tongue to say that there were no such investments, but I saw the warning look on the Fox's face.

In the meantime, the tax man continued to demand to be paid. When Prosperity just kept on begging, the tax man slipped a knife from a sheath on his belt and pressed the tip against Prosperity's arm.

"He's going to kill Prosperity," I said.

The boss explained that the tax man gets to keep part of the taxes he gathers. If he killed Prosperity, that was one less person to be taxed next month.

Finally, some of Prosperity's friends scraped together three dollars.

I don't think I'll be able to sleep tonight. I'll be hearing Prosperity's screams in my dreams.

I was just starting to feel comfortable here. Not anymore. We're in a strange country where they can do anything they want to us.

I wish I were home.

I wish I were safe.

July 18
Big Bend

There's another difference in American and Chinese calendars. This is a nice one. An American week has only seven days instead of ten like a Chinese one. The Americans call the seventh day *Sunday*. They don't work that day.

The Fox is following the Americans. He lets us have a day off every seven days. It's one American custom I don't mind.

That doesn't mean I've been lazy. This morning I've been writing letters for the other men. Uncle sat with me, mending the tears in my clothes. I think I could have done a better job of sewing. However, he said he wants to stand in for Mother as well as Father.

I have written everything in the letters from general wishes to stories that make me want to cry. Fathers wonder about their children. Husbands want to know why they have not heard from their wives.

They talk about their investments. (Real ones, not fake ones like Prosperity's. Some of them sound good enough to suggest to Uncle.) They tell me their plans on what fields to buy and what houses to build back in China. I hear all their dreams.

Prosperity was the hardest to listen to. He finally confessed to his family that he had gambled away all their money. There would be no more money for a long time. (I just wish I could have put his tears in as well.) His letter left me feeling tired.

That's when Uncle put his hand on my shoulder and said that I should enjoy my first day of rest in America. He was the opposite of Father, who could not stand to be idle or see either of his children idle.

I told Uncle that I'd work only until mealtime. I was really looking forward to that. We're going to have chicken for our big meal. The cook has been plucking them this morning. There are little white chicken feathers all over like flower petals.

So Uncle went off on his own. I hope I didn't hurt his feelings.

Later

I'm writing this during a short break.

At first, when I heard all the shouting in camp, I thought the tax man had come again. Then I saw Uncle moving toward me. He towered over the laughing crowd around him.

Then I realized he was on a horse! I can't exactly say that he "rode" the horse. His hands clung to the mane as well as the reins. And sometimes he sat on top of the horse, while other times he lost his balance and lay on his stomach on the horse's back.

The horse wasn't going fast. In fact it was plodding slower than a water buffalo on a hot summer day. When I asked Uncle where he had gotten the horse, he told me he had rented him from the drayer, and that we were going for a ride. Before I could get on the horse, Uncle insisted that I change my clothes. He gave me some parcels that had been tied to the saddle. There was an American felt hat with a soft brim, a warm coat and wool pants like Uncle's, and boots.

I caressed the clothes and boots. I knew they were expensive.

I could just see my father frowning at home when he heard about the extravagance. I tried to get Uncle to take them back.

Uncle said no. My father wouldn't want me shivering at night. I wouldn't do anyone any good if I died from the cold.

The heavy red flannel shirt fits fine and the pants can be taken up. The pants have pouches sewn inside them. The Americans call the pouches pockets. They're handy things. The boots are a little big, so we stuffed some rags into them.

After getting dressed, it was time for our ride. When I got on the horse, I had never before felt so tall.

Though we wanted to go to the top of the hill for the view, Uncle had trouble turning the horse, which clopped along with a mind of its own. To save his pride, I mentioned that the scenery here was pretty nice already.

Uncle seemed grateful as he let the horse pick its path. Tall trees grew on either side. Through the branches, I caught glimpses of the river. The sunlight reflected off the surface in hundreds of curving smiles.

I might have enjoyed the scenery more if I hadn't had to concentrate so much on staying on top of the horse. You wouldn't think a horse could be so slippery.

When I finally fell off, Uncle tried to catch me and fell off, too. That's why we're taking a rest. I just hope we can get back on the horse.

Afternoon

The strangest thing we saw today was in an open field. There were dozens of sticks crossed like the Chinese word for ten.

When I asked Uncle about it, he explained that the cross is a religious symbol and marks a grave. We were at an American cemetery.

Off to the side, a service was going on. A lot of the American miners were in their best clothes and their hair was slicked down. They were listening to a man speaking over a coffin beside an open grave. As I stared at the coffin, I thought again of Sunny. And of my cousins. And of Jubal's group. And of Hiram's brother.

I muttered something about how many died trying to get here. I felt Uncle's arms tighten around me and he asked if my crossing had been rough. It was the first time we had ever talked about it.

I thought of the cousins who had not made it to America. So I told him that his must have been rougher.

"It wouldn't have been my first choice." His arms were still around me as he held the reins. He gave my sides a little squeeze. "But I'm glad you're here."

There were a lot of people who would have babbled or shouted about feeling sad. We didn't do that in our family. We were too busy trying to survive. There wasn't time for complaining about how miserable we were. So that squeeze from Uncle meant just as much as days of praise from someone else.

Early evening

Uncle took me into town when he returned the horse. I wondered where all the people had come from because they hadn't been there before. Uncle explained that on Sunday, people come in from the surrounding claims.

And the racket! There seems to be a different dialect

for every person. There are all sorts of gambling games going on and the players shout out in victory or in misery. At the same time, there are men Uncle called tooters who are yelling and trying to drag passersby into the games. And there are lots of very "cheerful" men in tents who serve liquor.

From other tents I smelled meat cooking and saw men sitting shoulder by shoulder at crude tables. They were shoveling food into their mouths as fast as they could.

Uncle headed for the drayer's. It was a tent with a corral next to it. The owner was an American woman! She is the first I have ever seen. I think I stared a little too hard, because Uncle scolded me. The woman is named Mrs. Jones. She said she used to get a lot of stares from everyone. Women are still scarce in the entire province.

I like her. She has a good laugh, and she even gave me a piece of candy.

While Uncle finished his business with her, I went outside.

I felt sad at having to say good-bye to the horse and our afternoon ride. So I'm taking my mind off it by writing down what I've seen.

Evening

I had another scare.

On the way back to camp, I heard Hiram shout my name. I didn't recognize him at first. His old clothes were gone. Now he stood in boots and pants with the straps the Americans call suspenders. On his head was a hat with the brim turned up. There were even wisps on his chin as if he were trying to grow a beard.

I told him that he looked like a real miner. He said that I did, too. I guess I do, now that I'm wearing my new clothes. I introduced him to Uncle. Hiram wanted to talk, but before we could, a man came over angrily. He's a taller, older version of Hiram so I assume it was his older cousin. On his head was a cylindrical hat.

Hiram never got to introduce us. His cousin spoke too fast to Hiram for me to follow. Uncle, though, began to frown. So whatever the cousin said couldn't have been good.

I asked Uncle if Hiram was in trouble. Uncle said quietly that no, we were the ones about to have problems.

About thirty other Americans had begun to gather around us. Their faces reminded me of the bullies on the riverboat. And I realized what that face really meant. I'd seen the same expression on the cook's face when he twisted the chickens' necks.

I didn't mean that they were going to serve us for Sunday dinner. We were just animals to them.

All of them were wearing guns and knives, but there was no one to make them mind their manners. Suddenly I felt so alone. I stood as stiff as wood. Uncle grabbed my shoulders and turned me around toward camp. He whispered to me to walk and not show that I was frightened. It would only encourage them to do something.

As I shuffled forward, the jeering started. A lot of the words were words Hiram and Brian had never taught me. The tone, though, is the same one used by bullies everywhere.

Suddenly, a huge bearded giant blocked our way. He smelled bad, too. I tried to go around him, but he flung out an arm as thick as a tree trunk. Then he began yelling at us. I don't know what he said. All I could see were the rotted teeth in his mouth.

Hiram shouted something. Then he came running. His cousin chased him. The cousin's face was all red. Everyone seemed to be shouting at once.

The giant swung toward Hiram.

Uncle gave me a push while the giant was distracted. I wanted to stay with Hiram. Uncle kept pushing, though. "Your friend's all right," he said.

Hiram was surrounded by the bullies. However, all

they seemed to do was scold him. He saw me and waved his hand frantically for us to leave.

Still, I felt like an awful coward when I turned my back on him.

Uncle warned me not to look back to see if they were following us.

All I could do was force my legs to move one step at a time. But my ears strained for footsteps chasing us.

We didn't stop until we reached the edge of our camp.

When I asked Uncle what that was about, Uncle explained that the American miners blamed us for everything that had gone wrong in their lives — from lower wages to rain and warts. A month before I came, in other districts, the Americans threw the Chinese out. And some of the American miners here wanted to do the same thing.

Uncle says that this is proof that gold is a curse. It twists people's minds and makes them act like beasts.

I'm beginning to think Uncle is right.

I feel like shivering, but not from the cold.

America is so lovely — and yet so frightening.

◈ ◈ ◈

July 19

I felt the ride last night. I had to sleep on my stomach. Uncle had an ointment to rub on the sore parts. The soreness didn't excuse me from working, though.

July 20

I don't think the wing dam will ever get built. Uncle reminded me, though, that in northern China, Chinese built a wall all along the border. I should have remembered that from school.

The others have begun to call the wing dam the Great Wall.

July 23

Tomorrow is my reward for a week of hard work: another ride.

Uncle has promised me that we will take out the horse again. There are some waterfalls that Uncle wants to show me. With a little luck this time, the horse will cooperate.

July 25

So far no trouble in town this Sunday. I'm writing this while Uncle and I wait for the horse to be saddled.

We got up early and ate a quick meal. Uncle also got the cook to make up a meal to take with us.

I tried to hide my excitement as we reached town. A herd of twelve huge beef cattle were being driven into town for the slaughter. There were the usual Sunday crowds, but I didn't see Hiram.

Later

We've followed the stream to the falls. I could hear them long before I saw them. They cascade from a cliff in a huge tail of white plumes. The mist feels refreshing in the heat.

And Esteban is here! He and three men were on a rock with a basket of food. I guess they were having a picnic, too. When they saw us, Esteban's friends jumped to their feet and drew their guns.

Somehow Esteban and I managed to get everyone introduced. The three men are his brothers. They have come up for the day from their claim in the next district. They put their guns away with apologetic smiles.

There was so much I wanted to ask him. I'm sure he

felt the same way, but neither of us had enough words. I gather, though, that they too had met bullies like the ones we met on the boat and in town. I couldn't blame them for being fearful of strangers.

It was Uncle's idea to catch some fish.

I miss the fresh fish that we took from the pond at Tiger Rock. And I am sick of the salted fish we get in camp, so I agreed.

Uncle found some straight branches and stripped them so they were poles. Then he took a ball of string from his pocket. He must have been planning this all along.

I wondered what he was going to do for hooks, but he took out some nails and used a rock to bend them.

If Uncle was not successful at home, it was because of his bad luck, not because he was stupid.

He hummed happily to himself as he fashioned our fishing poles. Despite the growing dangers we faced working in the mines, I had never seen him so content. With all its risks, America suits an inventive person like him.

When the two poles were ready, he handed one to Esteban and one to me.

In the meantime, Esteban's brothers had begun to play a game with cards. As they tried to teach the game to Uncle through signs, Esteban and I dug worms out of the soil. Then we walked to where the stream still ran and sat on the bank and cast our lines into the water.

As we sat in the sun by the sparkling water, I forgot for a while about the American tax men and bullies.

Evening

When we got back to town, the casual crowd was gone and the bullies were out.

When we returned the horse, Uncle told me to stick close to him. After last Sunday, I didn't have to be told twice. As I tried to match his stride, I kept telling myself not to be afraid.

I was sure, though, that I could feel their eyes boring into my back like pick axes. Uncle acted like he was out for a stroll. He's like a whole different man here. I wish the clan back in China could see how much courage he has. Why hadn't I realized that before?

I hope America changes me, too. So far, I don't feel brave at all.

July 26

The bullies have gotten bolder. Today one of the miners went to town for supplies. A half-dozen bullies followed him out of the store and shouted insults all the way back to camp. They were like a pack of snarling dogs.

They stopped right on the edge of our camp. Then they saw us coming with axes and they scurried off.

The Fox ordered us all back to work, but he looks worried.

It's all anyone can talk about. Will we get kicked out like the Chinese in other mining districts?

Even Uncle, who always looks on the sunny side of things, isn't sure.

July 27

Uncle and a crew are cutting some of the smaller trees that are straight and true. I got to help with one of the two-person saws. It took a little getting used to it. American saws are the reverse of Chinese ones. Their saws cut on the backward or pulling stroke. Our Chinese saws cut on the forward or pushing stroke.

As soon as he had the first log, Uncle began to split it with wedges to make it into planks and smooth them with a plane.

◈ ◈ ◈

July 28

In China, water chains carry water from the stream to the nearby fields and irrigation ditches. They are wooden troughs with a chain of wooden paddles. No one else but Uncle knows how to build a water chain. Now I understand why he was hired at such a high rate.

Uncle and I have begun to construct water chains. He has only American tools, but once he got used to them, he seemed to forget about all our troubles. In between saw strokes, I could hear him humming. I found myself cheering up, too.

July 29

This afternoon one of the miners came back from town with a big lump on his head. The bullies had thrown stones at him.

As the Fox examined the lump on the victim's head, he said that this was a sign.

I couldn't see what of. At home, a sign would be like a certain star rising between the dragon's horns, which means it's time to start planting.

So I asked the Fox what he meant.

The Fox said just one word. "Change."

I thought the Fox meant he could read Wind and

Water. In China, there were experts who read the signs in nature. They could help make you rich and keep you healthy.

However, the Fox said that what he read was Americans. We have to be very careful from now on.

As if I need that warning.

July 30

Late this morning the Fox called everyone over. He had a letter to mail. Someone had to take it into town.

In the pre-bully days, everyone would have wanted the job as a break from work. Now no one did.

The Fox must have been expecting us to hold back because he already had straws in his back pocket. He told us that the one who drew the shortest would go.

He didn't want Uncle and me to take one. He needed Uncle to build the water chains, and I was too young. However, Uncle insisted on trying. I think he wanted to be fair to the others. And since Uncle did it, I took one, too.

I was sweating until I saw mine was a long one.

Naturally, Uncle's luck held true. He got the shortest.

I started worrying about those bullies in the town. With Uncle's luck, they will use bullets instead of stones.

Uncle's memory, though, is as short as his luck. He never seems to remember the last disaster.

He told me not to fret.

Of course, I can't help it.

Later

Uncle came back with his shirt all torn and cuts and bruises on his face. Well, at least he's alive.

The Fox tended to his wounds. When Uncle took off his shirt, I saw that his body had even more cuts and bruises.

He told us the bullies had jumped him after he mailed the letter. This time they had not yelled any insults first, so there had been no warning or chance to run.

I was all set for reporting them to the local magistrate.

The Fox stared at me as if I had said the dumbest thing. He told me it would be no use to go to the magistrate. Chinese are not allowed to testify in the courts. No one with a dark skin can. We are not people to the Americans.

When I asked, I found that Esteban and his brothers or Jubal would also not be allowed to be witnesses.

There are bullies not just in town and not just in the other mining camps. They are even in the government.

The Fox told me the whole truth then. If an American jumps one of our claims or robs one of us, it is not a crime. Not unless another American sees it and testifies.

I had never heard of a country with such laws, but the Fox said this is the Americans' country and their rules.

But it is our country, too. We work hard here and pay taxes. I thought of the bullies in the town. There are only a few of them. I expect most Americans are like Hiram.

The Fox agreed with me. Unfortunately, the good ones are just as scared of the bad ones as we are. There is no one to help us.

Suddenly, the Golden Mountain seems even farther away from home.

August 1

This Sunday Uncle didn't think it was safe to go into town to get a horse. I hadn't realized how much I looked forward to the rides. However, I tried to hide my disappointment.

Instead, I went to the edge of camp and tried to catch a glimpse of Hiram. I didn't see him. I hope he's all right.

I thought of what Uncle said about gold being a curse. I felt it reaching out with invisible hands to twist people's hearts and minds. It's made everyone crazy.

Uncle made more fishing poles for us so we could try our luck here. Of course, when the others saw me sitting idly by the stream, they came over to ask me to write letters, but Uncle chased them all away with a growl.

I thought longingly of the meadow and the waterfall. With the bullies about, it might just as well have been a continent away.

And what if they caught us there?

It's like the old story about the beautiful flower hiding the poisonous snake. When you're drawn to the loveliness, the snake strikes, killing you.

August 2

We have been busy building water chains. The faster we get to the gold, the faster we can go home.

August 5

The water chains have been set up in a row like insect soldiers. We'll move them into place when it's time.

Uncle and I have switched to splitting some of the smaller logs for wood. I work hard. I don't worry about the bullies when I'm busy.

August 10

This afternoon, the Fox sent a dozen men into town to see if a package had come. Naturally, Uncle got a short straw again. Prosperity's going, too.

The package must be important to pull that many men off the Great Wall. It must be as big as a boulder if you need a dozen. However, the Fox asked them to be careful because it's very fragile.

I can't work. I'm writing this as I wait near the edge of camp. I expect the worst.

Later

Uncle and the others got back safely. The others of the group must have had enough good luck to make up for Uncle's bad.

The package isn't the size of a boulder. It's a wooden crate that Prosperity easily carried by himself. Through the cracks between the boards, I could see wisps of straw.

They didn't have any trouble with the bullies. I guess twelve were too many to attack.

We were all dying to see what was in the crate. Everyone left work to gather around. So the Fox opened it right there. But we weren't to laugh and we weren't to ask questions.

When the Fox pried off the boards, he lifted out a huge chamber pot. He turned it around in his hands. There wasn't a chip on it.

I asked Uncle in a whisper why the Fox had gotten that.

All Uncle could guess was that the Fox doesn't want to use the latrines anymore at night. He figured that the Fox must be too scared to go out in the dark. The other miners think the same thing.

How can we work for a man who's too scared to leave his tent?

August 13

I was in the tent with the Fox when we heard the shouts of robbers.

I began to snatch up the coins of the payroll. I was going to run away. However, the Fox calmly told me to put them back down and step to the back of the tent.

I hated the thought of losing all our hard work. I told the Fox I could get under the tent side and escape with his money. The Fox snapped at me to do what he said. Hastily I dropped the sacks down onto the table.

Suddenly the flap was thrown back. Three robbers stood there. The cowards wore cloths over their mouths. Even so, their eyes and hair color said they were Americans. Beyond them I could see angry miners and my worried uncle. Two of the robbers stayed outside with drawn guns while the third strolled into the tent in broad daylight as if he didn't have a care in the world.

He spoke American when he demanded our money.

When the Fox got up, he put himself between me and them. Angrily, he ordered the robber to get out.

The robber hit the Fox so hard with his pistol that the Fox fell down.

I shouted in American for the robber to stop and to go away.

The Fox yelled back in Chinese for me to be quiet. Then he pointed to the table and told the robber in American to take the money and not hurt him any more.

The robber picked up the coins and stuffed them into his pockets. His laugh rubbed my ears like a plane on wood.

From outside, I heard the crew protesting angrily in Chinese and then a gun blast. I ran toward the tent flap.

Rising to his knees, the Fox tackled me and ordered me to wait.

"He shot someone," I said.

"Then you'd be hearing screams, and the camp would be stampeding to get out of their way," the Fox explained. "The robbers just shot in the air to make everyone back up."

Outside all I heard was anger rather than fear. The sound diminished as they followed the thieves out of camp.

Uncle came in to check on me.

For someone who had just been beaten and robbed, the Fox seemed very calm. He let me go and told Uncle that we were both all right and to go back outside.

The Fox had me bring him a jar of salve from near his sleeping mat. As I daubed the salve onto his cheek, he told me to listen to him next time.

I was stunned. They'd come back another time?

The Fox told me the robbers will come back like landlords after the rent. But with a little luck, the first set of robbers will be strong enough to keep other robbers away from poaching their personal preserve.

I didn't think it was fair and said so.

The Fox said we don't have much choice.

I remembered what he told me about the courts here. We can't complain because we aren't people to the Americans. I'd never felt more angry or helpless.

To my surprise, the Fox just chuckled. The thieves had gotten just dimes and pennies. Why did I think he stunk up his tent with the chamber pot? When the troubles started in town, he knew it was a sign to get ready.

So I told him what Uncle and the others thought was the reason: that he was scared to leave his tent at night.

The Fox started to laugh, but his bruise hurt too much and he had to stop.

He made me promise not to tell anyone — not even Uncle — what he was going to show me.

Then he reached into the chamber pot and pulled up a packet wrapped in oilcloth. This was his strongbox. That's why he had such a big chamber pot. They'd never look in there.

I'd been all wrong about the Fox.

"Where there's no law, you have to use your wits," the Fox said.

As the Fox cleaned his hands, he gave me a stern look. If we shoot any white man — even if he is a robber — we'll all be lynched. All the mob would care about is the color of the victim's skin.

And then he said something that I always want to re-member: "Remember, Runt. The real strong man doesn't fight back. The real strong man takes it and lives on. The family always comes first. Your ghost can't send them money."

Of course, I asked the Fox why he had fought for the gold then.

The Fox explained that he couldn't make the theft look too easy, or they would have become suspicious.

I see how the boss got his name.

He has a lot to teach me about being a guest of the Golden Mountain.

I just hope I live long enough to learn.

August 16

Such a crazy time. Everything has to be done in a hurry.

The crews are building the Great Wall out of the logs and planks. But the river hates being stopped. It keeps bashing at the dam.

Sometimes Uncle and the others have to go into the cold water. They shout and shiver as they hammer the boards against the logs.

They have to put their heads under the water since the logs are submerged. Also the water itself softens the force of their blows. And the icy temperature saps their strength. My hands go numb whenever I get water from the river. I don't think I could make it if I had to put my whole body in there.

The Fox has had to start setting them to work in teams. One comes out and the next enters the water to work. Then the resting team can dry itself off and warm up.

I stay on shore keeping a fire going and tea boiling so crewmen can dry off.

Have to get more firewood now.

Later

We nearly lost Prosperity. The river knocked him off his feet while he was working on the logs. One moment I heard the scream. The next I saw him already three meters downriver.

He managed to grab hold of a root, but the men near him wouldn't help. They just stood around shouting instructions to Prosperity and one another. I just stood there, too, with my mouth open.

The Fox himself ran to the rescue, his hat flying off. He looked a little funny, hopping first on one foot and then the other as he pulled off his boots. Then, grabbing a rope, he dove into the water.

Once again the Fox earned his name. He let the currents carry him to Prosperity. Then the Fox managed to get the rope tied around the waist of the drowning man.

When we hauled them both to shore, both were blue from the cold.

As soon as he had his breath back, though, the Fox ordered everyone else back to work. I was sent for blankets.

Prosperity was finished for the day and went back to his tent. The Fox stayed close by, supervising. The blanket was around his shoulders and the cup of tea between his hands. He was so busy shouting instructions that I don't think he ever drank it.

The Fox is an amazing man. He's brave as well as clever.

More than ever I feel like a runt. I just stood there and did nothing. I don't think I'll ever be a true guest of the Golden Mountain.

Still later

The first part of the wing dam is done. The last log didn't get set and nailed until sunset. There's still quite a bit of water flowing through.

The Fox walked across the top log and then splashed into the river itself. Every few steps his head would disappear as he dove to check the Great Wall.

When he had inspected the last piece, he announced that it would hold. Uncle fell asleep in our tent, too exhausted to eat.

I can barely hold my pencil to write these few words.

August 17

We're still working on the Great Wall.

August 20

This morning we began to haul baskets of soil to the river. The dirt is almost like clay, so it's heavy. We dump it over the face of the Great Wall faster than the river can wash it away. Then we add boughs that have been saved from the trimmed trees.

Even so, the river is determined to keep to its old bed. It finds cracks and sloshes inside. The water's still a meter high inside the Great Wall.

August 22

No break this Sunday.

We brought in Uncle's water chains and set them up. The chain gets turned by pedals. There is a stick in front to hold onto as you walk. Everyone takes a turn.

August 24

The water level has slowly been dropping behind the Great Wall. Now we can see the bottom of the stream. I crowded on the bank with the others, looking for gold.

When I saw specks at first, I thought I had found it. Then I realized they were moving around. We'd trapped some fish.

The cook stepped down from the bank in high boots. With his bare hands he began to snatch the fish and dump them into a basket. I guess we're going to have fresh fish tonight.

As I watched the silvery shapes fall one by one into the basket, I thought back to the time when Uncle had first marched out of Tiger Rock. I'd expected him to scoop up the gold just as easily.

That seems decades ago when I didn't know anything.

August 27

It's taken three days for the water level to drop. Uncle and I have begun building rockers. The Fox sketched diagrams on a piece of scrap wood for us. Rockers are boxes a couple of meters long and about a meter wide and about a quarter of a meter deep. There is a slight slope to the bottom across which cleats have been nailed.

One end of the box is open and a screen box is at the other a little above the bottom of the box. The screen box is a smaller one with holes through the bottom.

The whole thing rests on curved boards so it will rock back and forth. I guess that's how the machine got its name.

August 28

My first gold.

I slept only a few hours last night. Most of the camp was down by the river waiting for the morning.

When I reached the bank, I strained my eyes looking

for gold. It must be in small pieces or even dust. All I could see was the sun glistening on the mud. In dozens of places, I saw fish flopping about. (Fish again tonight.)

The Fox himself was the first to jump down with a shovel. Instantly he sank ankle deep in the wet mud and gravel. When he didn't dig right away, Prosperity shouted, "What are you waiting for? The gold isn't going to jump into your pockets."

The Fox just sniffed the air. "No, not yet."

To tell the truth, all I could smell was the mud. Some of it really stank.

The Fox is the Fox, though. He high-stepped through the mud and wet gravel until he was in the middle of the area behind the Great Wall. It was there his nose told him to dig.

Then he high-stepped back to the bank where a rocker stood. He dumped the test shovelful into the screen box. It didn't look like anything to me.

Then he dumped a bucket of water over it. The dirty water traveled down the angled bottom and gushed out the open end. I didn't see any melon-sized nuggets lying in the screen box. All I saw were small rocks and bits of gravel. I felt disappointed.

However, the Fox ran a finger along one of the wooden cleats.

And he announced to everyone that this is what they

had all come for. He held up a gleaming fingertip. The little flecks on it gleamed like stars. I don't think I have ever seen anything as pretty. I think I finally understand how gold can sink its claws into someone. I'll have to be careful not to go crazy, too.

Everyone let out a whoop and a roar. The sun reflected off the wet riverbed, so it shone as if it were all gold. Suddenly, it seemed like all our worries would evaporate like the mist rising from the mud.

August 29

No break again this Sunday. The Fox says we're in a race with the winter rains and snow.

After that first shovelful, there hasn't been any gold.

I remember when I was coming up here, I hoped I would get to see the snow on the mountains. However, we stopped below the snow line.

I'm still curious about seeing it.

But where is the gold?

August 30

Still no gold.

August 31

Will we ever find any more gold? All that work. All that sweat. Can it be for nothing?

September 1

Nothing but disappointment. The Fox has decided that the rest of the gold must be deeper. We will have to strip away the upper levels of gravel and mud.

We have begun to haul it away.

September 5

Though it's Sunday, there's no rest.

I feel so tired. After that first glimpse of gold, nothing. It's as if the land were teasing us.

We dig and dump, dig and dump.

September 9

The Americans are celebrating Admission Day. It's the day that California officially became a province two years ago.

The Fox says that's why there is so little government

here. Normally it takes longer for a territory to become a province. America was so eager to claim the gold that they made California a province right away, even though there were only a few government people to handle the rush of all those people, seeking gold.

Lots of guns going off. It sounds like a battle. They must be celebrating like they did on July 4th.

We've minded our own business and stayed in camp working. We're down half a meter. Still no sign of gold.

We hear the Americans haven't found gold at their dam, either.

Can Uncle be jinxing everything? Or maybe it's me?

September 14

Gold!

We had to go down a whole meter. All the rockers sway from side to side as we separate the gold dust from the dirt.

So far the robbers have not come back. Perhaps the Fox's plan is working. He has neither guns nor knives — only his wits. And yet he keeps winning.

As scary as this place is, I trust him to get us through the dangers.

September 18

We have begun to eat better. A wagon comes to us with fresh supplies from Chinatown now. We even get to eat with fancy chopsticks coated in black lacquer.

September 21

I feel like part of a machine. We scoop up the river bottom, dump it into a rocker, add water, and get the gold.

Every night I still can't rest. There are letters to write. And I have to help the Fox, too.

We dry that day's gold by a potbellied stove. Then we weigh it and enter the number into the ledger.

Some we put into a strongbox. Most of it, though, we put away in the chamber pot.

Strange, but the gold is always gone from the chamber pot the next night. It's like a beast that can never get full.

More of the Fox's magic.

September 24

The Fox stayed inside his tent all day fussing. He kept calling for more wood but never allowed anyone inside.

He must have the chills, because it's not that cold.

September 27

The three robbers came today. They took what was in the strongbox. The Fox wasn't acting when he protested. The robbers just laughed. Then they went through the camp, taking what they wanted. When they searched the kitchen tent, I was surprised at how many cases of lacquered chopsticks there were. I guess the Fox really likes them.

I hate the fact that these robbers can come into my home and take anything they want. But there's nothing I can do about it.

I remember what the Fox said. The family comes first. I won't do them any good if I get myself killed. But I'm still so mad inside, I hurt.

The sooner I get back to China, the better. We have laws there. Robbers go to jail.

September 28

It once thrilled me to get gold dust and nuggets. Now the little sacks are things we harvest. I get no more excitement than I would harvesting plums at home.

Why work so hard if the Americans are going to take it away anyway?

The Golden Mountain doesn't shine for me anymore. It's cold and gloomy and dangerous.

I wonder if a guest can stay too long?

September 30

Just when I think I know America, it surprises me.

It's grown cooler, and the aspen trees are starting to turn yellow. I thought they were dying. The Fox says they are just changing color. They'll lose their leaves soon but grow more next year.

Back at home, we must have trees that drop their leaves, too, but everything else stays green from the rains.

October 4

More and more of the aspen leaves have turned yellow. This morning when I woke up and went out to wash, I thought the whole grove had caught fire.

When the wind shakes the thin branches, the yellow leaves shimmer like flickering flames. Such a strange and beautiful sight. The others take it for granted. They don't understand why I stare at the aspens.

Even if I become an old guest, I hope I never get like that.

October 10

The leaves litter the ground like gold coins. They remind me of the ghost money you drop at funerals. Ghost money is gold-colored paper that fools ghosts. They're so busy trying to pick it up that you can take the coffin to the cemetery and let the deceased pass on safely.

Who are the aspen coins for? What ghosts are around?

I started to wonder whether I'll ever get home alive, or if they'll ship my bones home.

I feel terribly homesick.

Uncle says all guests get the feeling now and then. Sometimes at odd moments he hears a tune he heard in Tiger Rock. The only problem is that he can remember only half of the song. It nearly drives him crazy. He hummed it for me, but I don't remember it, either.

My homesickness works on me differently. Suddenly, I want fresh, leafy green vegetables. (I never thought I'd say that.)

I used to hate vegetables in Tiger Rock. That was all I ever got to eat. However, the diet at Big Bend is reversed. Here I eat mostly meat and rice with some pickled or salted vegetables.

In Tiger Rock, the water would have been drained from the rice fields by now and the rice would be turning a pale gold color. Everyone would be getting the vegetable seeds ready for planting.

Evening

I asked the cook to get me some seeds.

He asked me if I wasn't getting my fill of dirt by now. But then I realized he was teasing me. He promised to add seeds to the next supply run. He warned me that it is colder up here. The plants might not grow.

October 14

My seeds came today. I can't wait to plant them tomorrow morning. I'll get up at first light.

Night

I couldn't wait so I sneaked out of the tent and began to work by moonlight.

Uncle came out with a kerosene lantern and said we could work better with it.

I didn't think he had cared and said so.

Uncle said that people can't feel connected to the land when they just dig up gold. Creating living things in the soil is another thing. You can feel part of the earth again. That is something he has missed.

I guess I have, too.

October 25

The first green shoots have come up. The soil here is so rich. Back in China, the land is tired after so many generations.

I feel like I'm really part of America now.

The cook has promised to make a special dish for me. Several miners have asked me if they could have a taste. I guess they're homesick, too.

When I offered some to the Fox, he just warned me not to cook my meal till it was harvested.

October 27

I've been robbed!

My plants are gone!

The garden patch has been stripped bare. Who would have taken my vegetables before they were ready?

I just sat down in the dirt ready to cry.

The Fox came by and pointed at some tracks. They were the marks of deer hooves and rabbit feet.

October 29

I saw the deer before sunrise as I was washing up. He had returned to sniff around my vegetable patch. Angrily, I snatched up a stone and got ready to throw it as hard as I could.

However, it walked along so daintily that I stopped.

Wasn't I acting just like the American bullies?

The deer had as much right to be here as I did. We could share.

I didn't realize I had dropped the stone until I heard it thud on the ground. When I did that, I felt even more like part of this place. The deer and I were like cousins.

October 31

A bad storm last night. Lots of thunder and lightning.

Then I heard something rattle against our tent. It sounded like someone had dumped buckets of pellets. When I picked up one, I felt how cold it was.

Uncle said it was hail.

November 1

This morning I found two huge white birds in the water outside the Great Wall. They had black beaks with yellow spots in front of the eyes. With them was a smaller bird with gray feathers. The big ones have deep voices, but the young one makes high noises.

The Fox said they were swans. And the smaller one must be their child.

The cook was all for trying to catch one and cook it, but the Fox wouldn't let him. He said they were only trying to get home like we are.

The swans live up north in the summer and come down here in the fall before the snow comes. The Fox said that the storm must have forced them down here. They looked a little ragged and hungry after their long journey. The grown-ups began to preen their feathers as I watched them.

We have so much rice left over after a meal. It's such a contrast to Tiger Rock. I can remember years when I would eat every grain. Now I took a handful of cooked rice and squeezed it into a ball.

Then I went out on the Great Wall and threw it to them. It bobbed on the surface for a moment. The biggest swan sniffed it, then sampled it. The next moment he had gobbled it down. Then he made a loud sound that made me jump.

I fed them several more rice balls. Then I sat and watched them drift about the water, graceful as American sailing ships.

As they glided along, I thought of myself floating over the sea back toward home. It made me feel a little sad.

November 8

The whole camp has taken to feeding the swans. When they ran out of leftover rice, the men began to take the good rice as soon as it was cooked.

When the cook complained to the Fox, he ordered us to stop. He told us that if we keep feeding them, they'll be too heavy to fly out. They might even sink. They have to leave soon.

At first I was disappointed. I had wanted to watch them raise their young. However, the Fox explained that the swans had only stopped here to rest. They will head on to the Sacramento delta. The snow is coming.

I got excited about that. Finally I'll get to see snow. But Uncle grumbled, "You just wait. You'll wish you could leave with the swans."

November 11

The swans have left. It was quite a fuss.

I didn't realize how big their wings were. They must stretch more than two meters in length. When they flapped them, they began to splash the water. However, they rose only a little bit from the surface. Though they had their feet tucked in tight against their bodies, they dragged in the water. Finally, all three staggered up toward the sky.

It's made me feel sad again. Maybe because they can go on to their home so easily, and I cannot.

Or maybe it was because swans keep their families together. They don't send off the runts to die.

December 5

It has gotten cold — colder than I've ever known.

To keep warm, I go to bed in my clothes and jacket. All I have to do in the morning to get dressed is pull on my boots.

The cold makes it hard to work. The water numbs my fingers as soon as I touch it.

Every chance I get, I breathe on my fingers to keep them from getting stiff. And even though my coat would have kept me hot as a furnace in Tiger Rock, it feels as thin as paper here.

Uncle says it will get even worse, but I don't see how it can.

◈ ◈ ◈

December 8

It's raining, so no work today.

It was so cold I stayed in my blanket this morning, rolled up like a silkworm in a cocoon.

Though I don't work in the river, I'm still very busy. There are letters to write, and I have to help the Fox. He's teaching me how to read and write in American. So if Blessing had come, he wouldn't have gotten out of school after all.

I even try to read the American newspapers now.

December 9

Still raining, but lots to do. No word from home. I hope they're all right.

December 10

It's raining off and on. In one of the breaks, the Fox went down to check the level of the river by the Great Wall. So far it's still holding.

◈ ◈ ◈

December 19

It has rained now for five days.

Though it's not raining now, the sky looks like it will soon.

Something's wrong. The camp is too quiet for a Sunday. Is it robbers?

I'm going outside.

Later

It was Hiram and Brian. At first, I didn't recognize them as they stood on the edge of camp. They were all wrapped up in heavy coats and their faces were covered by mufflers. But they waved when they saw me.

Even so, I have learned to be cautious. I hung back until they called to me and pulled the mufflers away from their faces.

After the last few months, I didn't know what to expect anymore. Maybe the gold had driven them just as crazy as everyone else. Brian marched into camp, as friendly as ever. Hiram followed him a little shyly.

They both wished me a Merry Christmas, which is a big holiday for all my friends. Christmas will come next Saturday.

Brian had come up to visit Hiram. Esteban would come along later. He and his brothers had gone to church.

We were all starting to feel a little self-conscious because the other miners were staring at us. So we walked over to the Great Wall.

Thanks to the Fox's lessons, I can understand my friends better.

Brian asked about the water chains. I got on one and showed him how they operate. They both took turns pedaling.

Hiram said a waterwheel could operate a pump. We could get the water out more efficiently and faster. And he drew a diagram on the ground.

I'll mention it to the Fox.

Hiram's group, though, hasn't done well even with a waterwheel. They diverted the entire river down a channel and then built a dam across the river. And after all that effort, they have hardly found any gold. However, they have high hopes for next year. I didn't tell him how well we have done.

The Fox has said that gold likes to play funny tricks that way. He's heard of one company that hired teams of experts called geologists. They didn't find a thing on a claim, so they abandoned it. Then some man who could neither read nor write walked over the same area and tripped over a nugget. He tried to dig it out, but he kept finding more and more of it until it turned out to be a boulder as big as him.

We sat down by the river beneath the bare aspens. The ground was cold and hard, so we huddled up for warmth.

There was a lot to catch up on. Brian's claim has already played out and he has signed on with a hydraulic mining operation here. He doesn't like it much. If he had wanted to work for a company, he could have stayed at home.

Esteban joined us then. He gave me a holy card, a picture of a saint called Jude. He helps people with impossible causes. Esteban said he is the perfect saint for gold miners. He and his brothers have been praying to him a lot.

Brian and Hiram gave me a bunch of fresh new pencils. All I had from my last shipment was a stub, so they were welcome.

I felt a little guilty that I didn't have anything for them, so I told them to wait a moment while I got some tea for everyone.

I'm writing this now while I wait in the cook's tent. I'm going to trade him some letter writing for pieces of Chinese beef jerky. It's sweet as well as salty, so it's different from American jerky.

◈ ◈ ◈

Still later

They really liked the jerky. The cook even had some meat dumplings and other things to snack on.

While we ate, we exchanged news.

Esteban's having as much trouble as Hiram and Brian finding gold. So he and his brothers are thinking about trying their luck back in San Francisco. They can see that the ones who are really getting rich are the merchants, not the miners. Merchants can charge a fortune for just one egg.

Brian and I agreed that we dig up the gold, but that we don't get to keep it. Most of it goes to the storekeepers for food and other things.

Hiram, though, said Esteban was wrong. If the gold plays out, the stores' prices have to fall back to normal. The real money is in the land.

I thought of the rich fields we had passed on the riverboat. Some of them would have been perfect for rice.

If he can get a big enough stake, Hiram is going to try to start a farm here. He's seen how many American miners get sick from scurvy because they don't have fresh vegetables.

I asked him about his girl at home. Would she come out? If I loved someone, I don't think I'd ask her to risk that dangerous trip.

Hiram grew sad. His girl has already married someone else. So he has nothing to go home to.

It was strange to think of him turning his back on his homeland like that. I asked about his ancestors, but his grandparents are buried in an entirely different province, and his great-grandparents are overseas on a different continent.

That was even harder to understand. My clan has been at Tiger Rock for more than a thousand years. Many generations are buried in its soil.

Even the swans seemed to have more of a homeland than Hiram. Americans are so rootless. I almost feel sorry for them.

I asked him what his cousin thinks of his scheme. Although I would be sad to see Hiram go, secretly I was hoping that if his cousin left, so would some of the other bullies. Then it would be safe to travel about again.

However, the gold has its hooks into Hiram's cousin. He has vowed to live and die in the gold country.

Hiram looked guilty then and added that he is sorry about his cousin. He's tried to tell him what I am like, but his cousin won't listen. I could see how bad Hiram felt. I told him that I understand and that I wish there were more Americans like him. He answered that most of the town feels like he does, but his cousin and his friends shout so loud, they drown everyone else out.

Then I had a new worry. What if his cousin knew he was here? Hiram had just told him he was going for a walk. He didn't want to risk upsetting his cousin.

I was asking more about this custom of Christmas when we heard a commotion in the camp. It was another American. I didn't recognize him at first. However, when I saw the slips of paper in his hand, I figured he was collecting taxes.

It was too soon, though. When the Fox tried to protest, the American unhooked a whip from his belt. When he shook it out, it was as long as a man and as lethal as a cobra.

And when he cracked it on the ground, it threw up bits of dirt. Then he began demanding to be paid the taxes.

Hiram stared at him hard. He whispered to me that the man was no tax collector. He was another miner who had just lost money in a poker game with his cousin last night. He was just trying to cheat us.

When Hiram started forward, I tried to stop him because the other American might complain to his cousin. But Hiram was too angry. He ran forward waving his arms and shouting in American not to pay.

The bogus tax collector whirled around with a snarl. He recognized Hiram and threatened to tell his cousin.

Hiram wouldn't back down. If the bogus tax collector

did that, Hiram would tell the magistrate. Hiram was an American. He could testify in the court.

The bogus tax collector gave up then. He tried to pass it off as a Christmas prank — just a little something so he could buy some Christmas cheer.

As we sat down again, I asked Hiram if the bogus tax collector might get him in trouble with his cousin. Hiram said he was willing to take what came.

Brian and Esteban both offered Hiram places to stay if his cousin throws him out. So did I.

Though an icy breeze blew from the water and the tea had almost frozen, I didn't feel cold anymore.

December 20

The rain stopped, so we went to work. But it's SO cold. The mud is half-frozen, so it's slippery. We've all fallen a couple of times.

I told the Fox about Hiram's waterwheel. He said it might work for Americans, but not for Chinese. I can't understand why a clever man like him doesn't want better machines.

December 21

It's started to rain again.

December 22

Rain.

December 23

More rain. We keep hearing cracking and groaning sounds from the Great Wall. The river is swollen from all the downpours and keeps pounding with new strength.

December 24

It has been raining steadily for four days. The Great Wall finally gave way today. Timbers and planks went shooting down the river as it roared in triumph.

December 25

The Americans are celebrating their Christmas. Lots of shouting and singing despite the rain. They sound very drunk.

Evening

The Fox complimented me on last Sunday. I told him I couldn't take credit for what Hiram did. However, he said you can tell the quality of a person by the company that person keeps. I picked well, so my friends are always welcome.

And then he paid me the real compliment: I am becoming a true guest, so he can trust me.

He flipped up his straw sleeping mat and told me to help him dig. I got down on my knees beside him and began to scrape dirt out with him. A few centimeters below the surface was a large jar.

The strongbox and chamber pot are only big enough to hold a day's worth of gold. So he needed to store his hoard elsewhere.

When he opened the lid of the jar, I saw that it was filled with little sacks of gold dust and nuggets.

There were also all these molds for something long and thin. It took me a moment to realize they were for chopsticks.

The Fox hadn't been cold at all when he'd been burning all that firewood. He'd been changing the gold into ordinary-looking chopsticks. More Fox magic.

I got wood from the big pile outside his tent so we

could melt the gold down and pour it into the molds. When they had cooled off, we blackened them so they looked like lacquer chopsticks.

The Fox ships them out on the same wagon that brings in our supplies. He said that a couple of times, Americans have searched the wagon. However, he always puts real chopsticks on top. So far, all the boxes have made it to San Francisco.

I asked him why the Americans hadn't noticed how heavy fake chopsticks were.

The Fox says Chinese would notice because they use chopsticks all the time. Americans don't really know what they are.

Once again, I'm not to tell anyone. Not even Uncle. But I can tell you, diary.

I'm proud that he can trust me. I'm a little frightened, too. What if the robbers start beating me? I'm not as tough as the Fox. I'd tell them all his secrets after the first blow. I almost wish he didn't have so much faith in me.

When we had disguised all the gold, the Fox asked me what I was going to do when this job was finished.

I said I thought the city might be safer.

The Fox laughed. He explained that the city folk hate us just as much as the miners.

I said I thought it was rougher up here than in the city.

He admitted that that is true — for now — but what

will happen when every timid soul heads for the city? In no time, there'll be a hundred men for every job. It isn't dangerous up here if you use your wits. And he asked me if I had ever watched a deer.

I said I had just seen them by my vegetable crops.

The Fox told me to keep an eye on them the next chance I get. He said that deer eat when they can but they keep an ear and eye open. That way they can always slip away before trouble comes. That is the secret of a true guest.

The Fox did a little hop-and-skip dance step. He said a true guest has to be nimble of foot to stay on the Golden Mountain.

Real guests can't go running back to China, because China is no place for clever folks like us. In China we had to do what everyone told us to. On the Golden Mountain, though, we can become anything we want.

Then he took me outside the tent and took a deep breath like it was wine. We looked up at the night sky. It was full of stars. He told me the Golden Mountain casts a spell on a person. You can't shake it off.

Maybe that's fine for someone as brave and smart as the Fox.

But not for me. I'm still the runt.

January 1, 1853

We can hear the Americans celebrating their New Year's. Now I know what they do. They're shooting off their guns like they did on July Fourth and on Admission Day. I wish they wouldn't. It makes me nervous. What if they stop aiming their guns at the sky and start pointing them at us?

January 2

Snow!

When I first saw it, I thought it was feathers. I figured the cook was plucking chickens for our Sunday meal. However, more of it whirled by. It would have taken a whole flock of chickens to make that many feathers.

So I looked up. It was coming down from the sky. When one of the white things touched my cheek, it felt cold and the next moment it was wet.

Uncle told me the snowflakes were falling.

I tried to catch them on my palms, but the little dots melted as soon as they touched my skin.

I felt so happy I swung my arms back and forth. They went spinning every which way.

Uncle pretended to scold me. He said, What kind of Chinese wastes something to eat? Then he tilted back his head and opened his mouth. He looked like a little bird begging for food.

So I copied him. The snowflakes melted on my tongue. So that was what the sky tasted like. Cold. Sweet.

All around me, the other miners had started to lift their faces upward and were tasting the snowflakes.

The Fox grumpily told us to stop making noise.

But I'm writing this down now so I won't forget. I know Blessing will want to hear about it.

Later

The snow's still falling as I write this during our meal break. It's turned the trees into white balls of cotton and covered the ground. Since it's Sunday, I've been able to sit and enjoy everything.

I —

Still later

Sorry for the interruption but I was just beginning a new thought when something smacked my head. It felt cold and wet and knocked off my hat.

Naturally, I bent to pick my hat up. That made my backside a target. I got real mad then. However, as soon as I straightened up, I saw something large and white coming toward me. It kept getting larger until it struck me in the face.

When I wiped my eyes, I realized it was snow. A ball of snow whizzed by and struck another miner. Uncle was laughing. He spread his arms out wide and invited me to hit him.

I imitated some of the others and bent over and scooped up some snow. My bare fingers felt even more numb, but I flung it. It flew apart barely a meter from my hand.

"You have to pack it first, boy," Uncle said. He showed me.

By that time, snowballs were flying every which way. It looked like a startled flock of white pigeons were darting here and there.

Uncle stood patiently while I got more snow and shaped it into a ball. This time the snowball held together but my aim was way off.

At that point, I just gave up and did what some of the others were doing. I ran up to Uncle, squatted, and began to fling handfuls of snow on him.

The Fox came storming out of his tent to lecture us.

His hat flew off when he was hit with a dozen snowballs at one time. He rocked this way and that each time a snowball hit him.

Finally, everyone ran out of snowballs. We all stood watching.

The Fox wiped off his face. With great dignity he fetched his hat. Then he calmly walked right up to Uncle and me. I wondered if we were going to be fired.

As the Fox glared at us, he swept his foot, kicking up a huge spray of snow over Uncle and me.

Then snow was flying all over the place. Some grabbed shovels and began throwing snow that way. It was a wonder that the swinging shovels didn't knock out someone.

By the time we all paused for breath, I was feeling warm again from all the exertion.

Evening

The snow fell the rest of the day.

Tonight at dinner I took a cup of tea outside and sat on a tree stump. I hardly recognized our claim. The snow had softened the outline of everything. The hard lines of the rockers had disappeared under soft white curves. The whole world looked new.

When I went back inside, I wrapped rags around my hands to keep them warm. Otherwise Uncle said they could get frostbite as the Americans call it. Then we huddled together in the tent for warmth.

January 3

The soil in the riverbed has frozen. It blunts the pick axes when we try to chop it up. The Fox has ordered fires to be set on the riverbed to warm up the ground.

The water is so cold it makes my fingers ache. Everything is taking so much longer now.

January 6

The snow has already begun to melt. The trees, with their loads of melting snow, are miniature rain clouds.

I can't say I'll be sorry to see the snow go, though.

January 7

It got really cold again, so the melting snow froze. The trees are covered in icicles.

There is also ice on the ground. Everyone has fallen down at least once.

Things have slowed down so much, the Fox is almost tearing out his hair. He wants to begin the new wing dam.

January 13

Cold and miserable.

January 14

More cold. More misery.

January 24

It takes such an effort to do anything. The very air steals the warmth from my lungs.

Uncle was right. I've already had my fill of snow. I hate it. But I don't think I'll put that in a letter to Blessing. I'd rather have him stay envious.

Ha ha ha.

Year Three of the Era,
Prosperity for All

February 8

I've never had a New Year's like this. I've eaten so much food that I'm bursting. So many firecrackers I can't hear. I wonder what the Americans thought when they heard all the explosions. I bet we had more fun with our New Year's than they had with theirs.

Still no word from home.

Uncle says my father isn't the kind to send letters. That's for fancy folk. It doesn't matter that I write letters for guests all the time, and the guests are ordinary folk just like Father.

I'm not going to stop writing my family. It would be nice to get some news, though.

February 14

I've caught a cold. Uncle's worried that I might get pneumonia. I get to lie in the tent, but it's hard to think, let alone write.

February 27

I haven't been able to write for a while. My cold got worse. So this Sunday I've been moved into the Fox's tent, where a fire is kept going in the stove. But my cold doesn't get better.

February 28

It's so cold and gray and gloomy, and that's just how I feel inside.

Uncle and I play chess most of the day.

He said that if the clan saw him now, they really would think he was an idler.

I told him that everyone knows he isn't lazy. I caught myself before I said that he is just unlucky.

I think Uncle guessed, though, because he just smiled. He told me that whenever he feels tired or discouraged now, he thinks about home: Today's wages might buy a sliver of prime bottom land, or maybe a new chair for our house.

I saw what he was getting at. It is one step at a time.

He nodded and said, Before you know it, you've arrived at the gates of heaven.

I hadn't thought much about it before, but Uncle is good at explaining things.

I drank the hot tea he had brought me. Suddenly I started to remember all his other kindnesses since I arrived. He has taken such good care of me. He would have made someone a good father.

So I asked him how come he never got married.

Uncle said it wasn't for lack of interest. However, he looked so sad I asked him what had happened.

It turned out it was for lack of prospects. No one wanted to let their daughter marry someone with no luck.

I thought of my brother Blessing. He is tall and handsome. What girl wouldn't want him? But who'd want someone like me? I'll always be a runt.

Uncle said I am a guest of the Golden Mountain now. Families will care only about the size of my treasure chest. Mother will have to beat the girls away with a stick when I go home.

But who wants to get married, anyway?

Uncle just laughed and said he'll remind me of that in ten years.

He might have been right about the snow, but he was dead wrong about girls.

March 1

An American doctor came to see me several times. Now I seem to be on the mend. I've moved back to our tent, but I still get tired.

I think I'm going to stop writing.

March 9

This morning when I awoke I went outside to wash up. Ice had formed on top of the river in a thin layer near the banks. I had to break it to get to the water.

Suddenly, I heard a bird singing. It sounded so sweet.

Uncle came out of the tent and listened, too. He said that spring was finally coming, and it was about time.

I looked for the bird among the trees. That was when I noticed the little brown buds on the tips of the aspen branches.

I've done it! I've survived my first winter in America.

March 24

I love this land in the spring. The fields are all green after the winter rains. Flowers sprout everywhere. This morning I just stood outside the tent and smelled all the young, growing things.

I remember that smell. It's the planting smell. It's the time when you take the rice seedlings from the sprouting tubs. And the fields have just been flooded again, and they're waiting for us to plant the seedlings.

And you still have hope that everything is going to grow and your belly's going to be full that year, for a change.

Only this year, my family didn't have to worry. They had our gold.

April 1

The swans are back!

This afternoon they were floating before the Great Wall. I didn't feed them, though. I just sat and watched.

The young swan is now a pure snow white. He looks handsome. Too bad I can't change like him.

April 2

They left today, joining other swans high overhead. I heard a sound like *hoo-hoo-hoo*.

Uncle explained they were heading northward again. They have a home up there as well.

I hinted that the meadow by the waterfall is lovely. There ought to be all sorts of flowers blooming now.

Uncle said that he had been up there last year in spring. There would be songbirds, too.

I asked him if we could go. I could see that Uncle was tempted. However, to my disappointment, he finally shook his head. It is even more dangerous now that the Americans' claim has played out. They resent the fact that we're still getting gold from ours.

I argued that it isn't our fault they picked wrong. And anyway, it hasn't been their country for long. They took it from the Mexicans only five years ago. And the Mexicans took it from the Indians.

Uncle sighed and said that unfortunately, they don't see it that way.

As I watched the swans fly away, I wished I could go with them. It would be nice to leave all these crazy people behind.

April 3

This Sunday we heard shouting but I didn't recognize all the words. However, I did hear a crowd chanting something about how the Chinese must go.

Whether they knew American or not, the whole camp had fallen quiet. It was like listening to beasts roaring in a jungle.

I think we all thought about how far away China is. Even San Francisco seems too distant. We are alone here.

April 6

I've hardly had time to write in my diary. For the last three nights the Americans have held rallies just outside our camp. I haven't had time to brood, though.

Everyone wants to send a letter back home to China. They're so scared, they naturally think of home.

Sometimes it's just a few lines to tell their families how much they miss them. Most of them pour out all their worries and fears. I have to hear them over and over.

I try to be a machine that takes down their dictation. But sometimes I get very tired and very scared.

April 7

The Americans are meeting again tonight just outside our camp. This one is the loudest of all. A group of us have begun praying. I think I'll join them.

April 8

I can't sleep.

The Americans had another meeting. Their echoes

carried through the tents. I heard the word *kill* a lot. Sometimes I wish the Fox hadn't taught me American.

April 9

Today bosses from the other camps in the district came here. They've been talking with the Fox most of the day.

After they left, the Fox called all of us together to tell us what the bosses have decided to do if the mobs come to any camp.

Last May, mining districts all over the province drove out the Chinese. In some of those places, the miners were allowed to leave with their belongings. In others, they were robbed and beaten but still allowed to go.

In a few places, they would never leave at all except as bones back to China.

The bosses have decided that we should not resist if a crowd of bullies comes to chase us out.

Prosperity protested that the Fox is gambling with our lives. We should fight back.

The Fox told him that that would be even more dangerous. If we fought, we'd make the Americans even angrier and then someone would get hurt for sure. There was no way we can win against so many of them. Especially when there is no law to protect us.

I remembered what he had said about true courage — about how really brave people put their families before their pride. But it sticks in my throat. I'm like Prosperity. I want to fight. We made this claim.

However, I will obey the Fox. Somehow he'll pull off a miracle.

April 10

This Sunday the Fox just told us to pack.

I'm as shocked as everyone. We all expected him to come up with a way to hold onto our claim.

I used some names for the Americans that have no place in a high-minded journal like mine.

The Fox scolded me, though, saying that the Americans are people just like us.

That puzzled me and I asked him why he wasn't angry. The Fox admitted that he had been very mad the first time someone kicked him off his claim. I was amazed he had stayed up in the gold country after that.

He held up three fingers. The Americans had jumped three different claims. Twice in his first year here and then again in his second.

I scratched my head at how calm he was about it.

He told me that hate is a luxury for a guest. Hate is so much baggage that slows a guest down. And a guest has to be nimble. He tapped one foot against the ground to remind me.

I pointed out that Americans hate us.

The Fox explained that they hate us only because they are scared of us. And they are scared for their families just like we would be.

But I swore that I will never forgive them.

The Fox told me I don't have to. I just have to go on with my life.

April 11

The Americans held another loud meeting. It sounded like a bunch of lions roaring. I thought for sure they were coming to drive us out.

I helped the Fox bury the chopstick molds. He must really be expecting to leave.

April 12

Still nothing. The waiting is getting on everyone's nerves.

April 13

This has to be quick, but if something happens to me, I hope my diary survives. The mob is coming. I'm so scared.

April 19

We've been running and hiding for six days.

I can now write more about the day we left because the Fox says we're safe for the moment. We're taking a short rest. While the cook brews up some tea, I want to write down everything before I forget.

Today started out like any other. We worked on the claim and then went back to clean up.

Just as I was washing, Hiram stumbled onto the claim. He was sweating and panting as if he had run all the way. He told me we all had to get out. A mob was coming to drive us away from the claim.

The miners who understood American began to tell the others Hiram's news in hushed, frightened voices.

I knew Hiram had taken a considerable risk to come here, so I thanked him. Then in the same breath I told him to leave. I didn't want his cousin to catch him here.

Hiram shook his head and said it didn't matter. He wasn't going to stay. He'd lost his taste for mining. He'd try his hand at farming that rich land we'd seen on our way up here.

There was so much we wanted to say to each other, but there was no time. A miner shouted from the edge of our camp that the Americans were coming.

I said that maybe I'd drop by his farm sometime. With

a grin, he told me I'd be welcome. I watched him slip into the brush near the camp. Then I went inside to get my things. I hid my diary in my pants. It was the one thing I didn't want to lose.

When the mob finally came, they had torches, so I could see the bully faces in front. Behind the front rows, the faces looked different. Many looked embarrassed. They didn't seem to want to be part of the mob.

The Fox reminded us again to stay calm and not fight back. Then he announced to the mob in English that we were leaving.

A dozen Americans began to grab our things and go through them. They began to take some stuff. Some of the Americans, though, were ashamed and pulled the looters back. We gathered up our scattered belongings, including the disguised gold.

The mob kept the strongbox, but there was only a small amount in it.

As I stumbled into the dark, all I could think was, Who will feed the swans?

Later

We're taking another short rest. I should sleep but I can't.

I should be glad to escape a place so deadly. And yet I feel as sad as when I left Tiger Rock.

I haven't been here a year and yet I've come to think of Big Bend as home. And all the animals as my kin. Sometimes the land is so beautiful it takes my breath away. And the thought of leaving it makes me ache inside.

If only we could get along with our neighbors.

Still later

Leave it to the Fox. He's already come up with a new plan.

He said the gold is getting too hard to find, and once you find it, it is even harder to get it out. It takes hydraulic equipment, and only a big company could organize that. I thought of the huge hose carving out the mountainside that I had seen on my way up.

Prosperity suggested setting up a really big company with that kind of equipment. A lot of people know the Fox has a nose for gold. They would invest in his company.

The Fox said he knows ways to find gold more easily. The trouble is the Americans. If we put in too many improvements, we would just make ourselves an even more tempting target for some group of claim jumpers.

However, the Fox insists that there is other work for us in this province. He has heard that the Americans want to build levees and reclaim some of the Sacramento delta. The mountains have been pouring rich soil down the river for years. But that kind of work is too hard for Americans. Though it might not pay as well as mining there would be a lot of jobs for Chinese.

That's cheered up everyone. We'll still be able to send money home. It's not going to pay as much, but it'll still be something. And American money will still be worth much more in China.

The real important thing is that the American bullies won't be jealous.

What had the Fox said? One step ahead? He was dancing on nimble feet way in front of everyone else.

April 22
Califia

We're safe. We're in another district called Califia. The Fox says that in the first few months of the gold rush, the hoards of miners stripped the gold from here. There are hardly any people in the district, American or Chinese.

All of us are breathing easier.

Uncle, though, is strangely quiet. That's a bad sign.

April 23

We followed the river all day without seeing anyone else.

It's like the end of the world. The only signs that

humans had been here were the rotting rockers and ruined shacks.

We've camped for the night on an abandoned claim. The shack's roof is gone. A broken rocker sits beside the bank. Holes dot the banks. It looks like a battlefield.

The bank juts out like a finger, forming a breakwater. The river forms a lazy eddy behind it, which the Fox said would be a good spot for gold to drop out.

It's a good thing we've stopped, too. My feet are so sore that I soaked them in the river. For once, I'm grateful the water is icy cold.

Uncle sat like a lump beside me. He said he didn't see how we'd ever get really rich piling up dirt for levees. It's like we're in prison and every day we have to do hard work.

I reminded him of what the Fox said — that we'll still be sending home something. It might be less but it will still be a lot by Chinese standards. But Uncle just kept staring at the river.

The cook fixed a quick meal. Since we can eat only what we could carry away, everything's rationed. The meals are small — about what they'd be back in China.

But we're alive. That's the important thing.

April 24

I can hardly write these words. Uncle's left me.

This morning he told the Fox that he was going to stay and prospect. He bought his own ticket here, so he was free to leave like any employee. The Fox didn't need a carpenter anymore.

The Fox thought he'd lost his senses. After all, we'd just gotten chased off our claim by a mob. Uncle might not survive the next mob.

Uncle said he would search around here for a new claim. The Fox had said it was safe enough.

The Fox tapped his nose and said, "That's because there's no gold, or this would have told me."

Uncle has plans for home. He can't carry them out piling up dirt.

The Fox shook his head but suggested that I go with him.

I was scared at the idea of staying in the gold country. However, I thought of Uncle left alone in the mountains with his bad luck. He wouldn't last a week.

So I said I was going to help Uncle.

Uncle tried to use his authority as the head of the family and tell me to go with the Fox.

I refused.

Uncle said I was useless to him. He didn't want me hanging around his neck anymore like a stone.

I started to cry. Even if Father and Mother didn't need me, I had been sure Uncle did.

Uncle kept saying a lot of hurtful things. I tried to remind him that he had been glad when I came.

He insisted that had been a lie and said I was nothing but a burden on him.

The Fox came over and put his hands on my shoulders. As we walked away, he told the cook to leave some supplies and a few tools with Uncle.

The others made their farewells to Uncle, but I stood by the path ready to go. When we left Uncle, I didn't even look back.

We've made camp for our noon meal. However, I've had no appetite. I have to talk to someone, even if it's only my diary.

How could Uncle say those things? How?

Evening

I am writing this quickly by moonlight. I tossed and turned for hours. I can't let Uncle die in the mountains. Even if he doesn't love me, he is still family.

Everyone is asleep. I'm going to leave a note for the Fox and then sneak away and find Uncle.

April 25

About an hour after midnight last night, I reached the shack where we had left Uncle.

Uncle was sitting by the river. His shoulders were silvery in the moonlight.

I hesitated, expecting him to say more hurtful things. However, I'd had time to rehearse a speech. So I told him I'd try my best not to be a burden.

Uncle came rushing toward me before I could finish. He gave me a big hug. He told me he hadn't meant what he said.

I asked him why he had said it then.

Uncle thought I would be safer with the Fox. Those hurtful words were maybe the hardest things he'd ever had to say.

I'm not ashamed to say that we both wept. When we finished, we decided to look for gold in the morning.

To change our luck, I spun on my heel and recited, "Spin around, turn around, luck changes."

With a chuckle, Uncle copied me.

When we entered the shack to go to sleep, I had to laugh. There isn't any roof. We might just as well sleep outside.

However, the shack does have a fireplace. After we

had gathered branches, I got a good fire roaring in the fireplace. Then we lay down in our blankets.

As I stared at the flickering flames, I thought of Mother. I used to squat by the front of the stove feeding the fire while she cooked. She used to like to hum, and the flames seemed to dance to her tune.

When will I see her again?

Later

Just had the worst nightmare. The mob was chasing me. I tried to run, but there was mud all around. I kept slipping and sliding and the mob kept gaining.

I must not have slept for very long, though, because the fire is just now dying. There are little dots of light all over the dirt floor of the cabin. They look like the torches the mob carried.

We're safe. We're safe. For now.

Still later

I'm trembling so badly I can barely write these words.

As I stared at the glittering floor, my curiosity got the better of my fear. What was reflecting the light?

So I crawled out of my blanket and crept across the floor with my nose almost touching the dirt.

I smelled gold. After spending all that time drying it and weighing it with the Fox, I know its smell by now.

That's it. Drying it!

The owner of the claim probably got the gold from the river. That means he had to dry it at night just as the Fox did with his gold.

There is gold dust scattered all around us.

I've got to wake Uncle and tell him.

Night

When I first told Uncle my theory, he didn't get excited.

Instead, he said it was an interesting idea, but why didn't the owner pick up the gold?

I said that maybe the light had to be just right from the fireplace.

Uncle looked thoughtful. He admitted that he hadn't noticed it when he first came in here. And it had still been day then.

I tried another explanation. The Fox had said this area had been worked in the early months of the gold rush. There was still plenty of easy gold then.

Uncle eagerly agreed. He said that maybe the owner thought the floor wasn't worth the time.

I said that the owner had probably thought there would be nuggets just waiting to be picked upriver.

"Maybe even big as melons," Uncle had to laugh.

His boast in the village seems so long ago now.

We'll wait until sunrise. One of the walls should give us the lumber to build a rocker. Then we'll know.

I don't know how much sleep I'll get, though.

April 26

It took half the day to build the rocker. Then Uncle dug up a shovelful of soil by the fireplace. Carefully he carried it over to the rocker. I used my hat to pour water in.

Gently we began to make the rocker sway. Water ran through the holes at the bottom.

Then we held our breaths as the water poured out.

Uncle got discouraged right away when he didn't see anything.

I leaned my head this way and that, studying the wooden cleats from all angles. "Wait," I said. There was a faint gleam of light.

I ran my fingertips along the edge and held it up. Bits of gold clung to it.

April 27
Evening

We're rich!

It took only one and a half days to get a small pouch of gold! Uncle says we'll make our melon-sized nuggets the hard way, one flake at a time.

April 29

We went into town to buy supplies and tools like pails and things, but we were careful not to bring too much gold with us. Uncle let me do the talking since I've learned more American than he has.

The Americans laughed at us when we registered our claim. Then they told us there is no gold up there.

Uncle was curious when I insisted on buying a big chamber pot but he gave in.

Later, when I told him what the Fox used his chamber pot for, Uncle had a good chuckle.

May 4

We've cleaned out the cabin floor.

Uncle says our method of mining is worth more than the gold itself. We have to protect it.

I agree, so we've filled in the holes and smoothed over the dirt floor with branches. When we were finished, it looked just as we had first seen it.

Now it's on to the next abandoned claim.

May 24

We stop only at abandoned claims where there was likely
to have been gold at one time. Uncle and I have picked up
a lot from the Fox and his nose for gold. We look for spots
where the river widens and the water slows, or behind
breakwaters like our first claim. Sometimes we look inside the bends of the river or in the pool of slow water
that forms just before the rapids.

So far we've tried ten more abandoned claims on this
side of the river. Not every miner was careless, but two
more have paid off. One of them was the richest of all.

Every time we file a new claim in town, they laugh at
us some more. We're just the crazy Chinese to them.

We just smile.

While we work, I tell Uncle about some of the invest-
ment schemes I heard from my friends and some of the
miners' letters. Uncle agrees with me that a store might
be a good idea sometime in the future.

Uncle says that maybe once we have the store, we'll
bring some of our cousins over from China.

May 26

We're going to take our gold into Sacramento. It's time to
bank it.

May 27
En route to Sacramento

It's so strange to be riding a wagon back to Sacramento. The wagon's going directly there, so the trip is much shorter than when I first went into the gold fields.

Our gold is in a basket that I'm sitting on. No one looks twice at two dirty, raggedy guests. And we muddied up our basket to look just as run-down as us.

The hills are green from the winter rains. In the dells where the water gathers, flowers are blooming. I think you could grow anything here.

Hiram's right. It's the soil here that's the real gold in America. Once the metal's gone, it's gone. The earth will keep bringing up new crops each year.

I wonder what happened to Hiram and his dream of a farm?

May 31
Sacramento

I am writing this while the clerk in the American bank finishes weighing and recording our deposits.

When we arrived on the wagon in Sacramento, I saw that it was all new. About a month after I came through here, a terrible fire burned down everything.

When we opened our basket in the American bank, the bank clerk was very curious. He kept wanting to know if we had made a big strike. On the way down here, though, Uncle and I had already decided to just smile and say as little as possible.

Once we get our bank draft, we'll go over to Chinatown to the headquarters of our district back in China.

Then we can send some of the money in the American bank back to China. I wish I could hear the clan when our money gets there. They'll say Uncle must have luck as big as a mountain.

Later

I am writing this in the boardinghouse. It's in Chinatown, but it has real American beds! No straw mats on the floor. The bed is as soft as a cloud. Finally I feel rich.

The room is above a restaurant. Such wonderful smells are coming from the kitchen. My mouth is watering.

Uncle says we're going to order everything on the menu and a lot of things that aren't.

Guess who we bumped into at the district headquarters? The Fox was sitting in the office doing some business.

His jaw dropped, and he stared at us like we were ghosts. Uncle promised him we were real enough.

The Fox shook his head in disapproval. He thought we must be starving because we are so bony.

However, it is my cooking. I am better at finding gold than at making meals.

The Fox looked like he felt sorry for us. He urged us to work for him on the levees. All our friends are doing well.

Uncle winked at me and told the Fox that he'd think about it.

The clerk just curled his lip up at us. He didn't even offer us a chair.

However, when Uncle handed him the draft from the American bank, the clerk's eyebrows shot up. He held the paper up to the window and studied the signature every which way to see if it was a forgery.

Uncle told him to check with the bank. The clerk immediately sent an assistant scooting over there. In the meantime he offered Uncle a seat. This time he called Uncle "sir."

When Uncle demanded a chair for me, the clerk got up and gave me *his* chair!

Soon the assistant came back from the American bank. Our draft was good, he told the clerk.

The Fox had stayed in his seat. Now he leaned over and sniffed us. "I smell gold."

Uncle said truthfully that there is nothing left in the rivers.

The Fox wondered if Uncle had found the secret of turning rocks to gold then. Uncle just complimented the Fox and said he had taught us well.

The Fox took off his hat to scratch his head. He couldn't have been that good a teacher if he didn't have a clue as to what he had taught us.

We had outfoxed the Fox!

When Uncle offered to take him to dinner later, the Fox accepted but said he'd rather know the secret.

Next we ordered some food and supplies. Then the clerk nodded politely to Uncle's ragged and patched coat and informed us that the store carried a full line of clothing.

Uncle fingered the worn material of my sleeve. I could see he was weakening.

However, if robbers see us in new clothes in the gold fields, they will come after us. I whispered to Uncle that if we show up in Califia with new clothes, we'll wind up being buried in them.

So Uncle sighed and told the clerk not yet.

As the Fox said, a guest has to be nimble of foot.

Then we told the clerk that we will pick up our purchases in a few days. After that, we checked into the boardinghouse and had baths. Uncle figures we can be clean while we're in Sacramento — even if we have to get dirty again before we leave for the gold fields.

Then we went to the barber. Uncle had a shave and

we both had the crowns of our heads shaved and the sides trimmed. We even had the wax scooped out of our ears. The real deluxe job, just like rich gentlemen!

After that, Uncle disappeared on some errand, so I went back and asked the clerk if he could ask his contacts in San Francisco if they could find Esteban and his brothers. I was hoping that they had started a store there. If I can find Esteban, perhaps I might find Hiram and Brian, too.

July 22

I have to apologize to you, diary. I've been so busy that I haven't had the time to even open your cover.

By now we have tried thirty abandoned claims. We worked up one side of the river and then back down and along the streams. Three of them paid off.

Today Uncle said it was time to go back down to Sacramento. I was all for trying another claim a kilometer to the north. Uncle said that it could wait. We were already a month late in celebrating an important anniversary.

In my mind, I ran through the American and Chinese calendars. I couldn't think of a festival, so I finally asked.

Uncle tapped me on top of my head. It's the anniversary of my arrival on the Golden Mountain!

Has it been a year?

It seems like just yesterday I was standing by Tiger Rock wishing I could stay.

July 28
Sacramento

When we got to Sacramento's Chinatown, the clerk was all smiles the moment he saw us. We're old "friends" now.

Uncle surprised me when he said it was time for a new wardrobe for himself and me. The clerk started rubbing his hands together and promised he would wait on us personally.

I tried to protest that it was too soon to quit. However, Uncle told me firmly that it is time. The Americans in Califia are starting to get too suspicious. We aren't going back.

I thought of all that gold still lying around on the floors of all those abandoned shacks. And I begged for one more month.

Uncle reminded me that we wanted what the gold can buy, not the gold itself. And we now have enough to do that.

Uncle's right, of course.

I guess I did get the gold curse. It's a real sneaky thing. I caught it without knowing it.

Noon

New haircuts and new outfits. I don't recognize myself in the mirror. Uncle has promised me that we'll have our pictures taken so we can send them home.

Later

We went to a man the clerk recommended. Though he's American, he has Chinese costumes, so he must have done this for other Chinese. A lot of the stuff is what a rich Manchu would wear. I didn't want to put it on, but Uncle said a rich man is a rich man. So I've humored him.

I'll have to apologize to Piggy if I ever see him. There really are cards that capture faces. Or rather, it's not a card but a plate. Later, the image from the plate can be transferred to cards.

Evening

The clerk has given me Esteban's address. He's in a town called Monterey. I'm going to write him tomorrow.

There was a letter from home, too. Finally.

Uncle saved it until we had dinner. Over tea and fruit in the restaurant, Uncle opened the envelope. Inside was a letter wrapped around another envelope. He gave me that page because it had my name on it.

As Uncle read the gossip in his letter, he chuckled occasionally or muttered something. Puzzled, I opened my envelope and unfolded the letter. The first part was from Mother:

> *Dear Bright Intelligence,*
>
> *We are writing this letter to you through the kindness of your teacher. When you read this letter, it will become obvious why we could not use Blessing to write it for us.*
>
> *Your uncle has told us about your clever scheme and what you have done for all of us. I am so proud of you.*
>
> *When your father decided to send you overseas, I argued that neither of my boys should go. However, he reminded me of what a warrior you are.*
>
> *When you were born early, you were so tiny that the midwife did not think you would survive. But you fought to live.*
>
> *I love you and miss you very much. Come home soon.*

So I wasn't nicknamed after the runt of the litter. It was because I had been born too soon.

The next part was from Father. It began with a warning:

Whatever you do, do not let Uncle read this letter.

I knew if anyone could keep your uncle alive, it would be you. You and Blessing remind me of myself and your uncle when we were young. I've always had to watch out for him, just as you have looked out for Blessing.

But you've far exceeded our hopes. Not only have you kept your uncle safe, but you've helped him make a fortune.

In a letter, I can't tell you how much we love you or thank you enough. Now that we're rich, we want you to come home. Of course, it has to be all right with your uncle.

I have been so wrong, thinking that they didn't love me. So why do I feel like crying?

Uncle was curious about my letter. So I carefully read him the safe parts. Later, when I had some time to myself, I could read it again.

When I was finished reading my letter to him, Uncle looked sad. He said I should go home since my parents want it.

For a whole year, I've been wishing to go home to China. I should be happy. But for some reason, I feel an awful ache inside.

It's ten times worse than when we fled the Fox's claim

and I thought I'd never see the gold country again. And it is a hundred times worse than when I left Tiger Rock.

It's crazy to feel this way.

Still later

Back in our room, I remembered that Uncle had said that *I* could go back. He didn't say *we*. So I asked him if he was returning to China, too. Uncle said he's going to open up the store and maybe look around the Golden Mountain a little more.

He told me he'd gotten itchy feet. He'd like to know what's around the next hill and the next bend in the river.

Evening

I can't sleep. I keep remembering all the good people that I've met here on the Golden Mountain. And I've thought of the waterfalls and meadows and other wonders I have seen. Those are the real treasures. Not the gold.

The Golden Mountain is like some food from a fairy tale. It fills you up wonderfully, but it always leaves you wanting more.

And there are my friends, Hiram and Brian and Esteban. I'd miss them as much as I missed my clan at Tiger Rock. Maybe more. We are all dreamers, and we are all risk takers. They are my clan in spirit if not in blood.

And though they came here only to get rich, they stayed to sink their roots. I'd feel like a coward if I went back to China now.

It's strange how things get turned backward on the Golden Mountain. Like the sawing stroke. Like the writing.

Like my feelings.

Night

I'm too excited to sleep now. I keep thinking about what life would be like in Tiger Rock. There would be my books. But there a rich person can't ride on a horse to waterfalls and meadows of flowers. That wouldn't be dignified.

There are a lot of things rich people aren't supposed to do in China. You can't even scratch when you itch. That kind of life would be tighter than a too-small jacket.

Here on the Golden Mountain I am free. I can scratch all I want. And I can get all the books I want from San Francisco.

I remembered what the Fox said that Christmas night. The Golden Mountain had caught me, too.

I wondered if this is how the swans feel when they leave one home for another.

And then it hit me.

The swans have two homes. Why can't I? Maybe I'll go home for just a short visit. Then I'll come right back to the Golden Mountain.

I feel guilty about that. And a little scared, too. I've never disobeyed my parents in my life. And yet it was they who sent me here. I can't help it if the Golden Mountain has gotten into my blood. I'm not just their son. I'm also a guest now.

July 29

This morning I told Uncle I want to go back to China for only a brief time. I really want to come back to him.

He warned me that my parents will be upset, maybe even angry.

But I told him it doesn't matter how mad they are. He is still the head of our family. If he orders me to return to the Golden Mountain, my parents will have to go along with it.

Uncle gave a big sigh of relief. He said he'll do just that. All I have to do is send him word when I want to come back to America. After all, he is used to having my parents scold him. He'll take the blame. And be glad of it because he wouldn't know what to do without his partner.

I don't know either.

Epilogue

Runt returned to China. Though he had intended to be there for only half a year, his parents kept finding excuses for him to stay. So they drew out his "short visit" to four years. Unfortunately, Uncle Stone was right about Runt's marriage prospects. Now that he was rich, many families were interested in him as a groom. Though he was still young, families began to ask about a possible match. Frantically, Runt got Uncle Stone to order his return to the Golden Mountain. Safely back in San Francisco, he met the native-born daughter of a Chinese merchant in Chinatown. When they were both eighteen they married and began to raise a large family. Runt never went back to China.

Runt's language skills, knowledge of other cultures, and friendships with non-Chinese made him a key figure in Chinatown. He was active in fighting the anti-Chinese laws that America began to pass. In Chinatown, it was said that though Runt never grew very tall, he cast a giant shadow.

Uncle Stone never did go back to China, but stayed in California. He started numerous business and banking ventures, but he always sold his interest so he could start his newest scheme. As a result, he never stayed with any of his enterprises long enough to reap the fruits of success. Nonetheless, Chinatown respected him, as a man with foresight. It was said that without him half of Chinatown wouldn't have come into existence. He always had a place at his nephew's table.

Though Blessing never got to come to the Golden Mountain, three of his sons became guests.

The Fox and his crew helped reclaim some 217,000 acres from the Sacramento delta. He later became a labor contractor, supplying Chinese workers for the many industries and farms that were starting up all over the West. He provided some of the 12,000 Chinese who helped build the transcontinental railroad. One of those was Prosperity, who then went on to help build many of the railroad branches. He never did repay what he owed the Fox, though.

The Golden Mountain cast its spell on Runt's friends as much as it did upon him. They all stayed in California. Though Esteban's brothers returned to Chile, Esteban stayed in Monterey, where he worked his way up at a small hotel until eventually he owned it. Throughout, he retained his love of fishing and could often be found along the rivers or coast casting out his line.

Brian chased various silver and gold strikes around the world. Good fortune always eluded him, however, until he came back to San Francisco. There his friendly ways made him a successful politician.

Hiram became a farmer, finally settling in the rich fields of the Sacramento delta that the Fox and his crew had helped reclaim. He remained a staunch friend of the Chinese even in the middle of the anti-Chinese riots of the 1880s. He defied mobs and refused to fire his Chinese hired hands though his barn was burned down twice.

Jubal and his master quickly ran into trouble in the gold fields. The American miners objected to working alongside a slave. After trying several districts, his discouraged master released Jubal, who found his way to San Francisco. There he apprenticed himself to a tailor. Later, he published his own newspaper, *The Elevator*, devoted to African-American issues, and established friendships with several of San Francisco's literary figures.

Life in America
in 1852

Historical Note

On January 24, 1848, James Marshall discovered gold while constructing a sawmill for Captain John Sutter. Since John Sutter's goal was to build his own colony in California, he and James Marshall tried to keep it secret. However, word leaked out and by the summer, cities like Monterey and San Francisco were deserted. Everyone had headed for places such as Coloma and Sonora and Hangtown (later renamed Placerville). Back east, people were skeptical until President James K. Polk confirmed the reports on December 5. Suddenly the rush was on.

Since there was as yet no transcontinental railroad, Americans were forced to choose among several dangerous routes to California. One sea route went all the way around South America, but the storms at the tip, Cape Horn, often proved deadly. The shorter sea route was no less risky. Would-be prospectors landed on the Atlantic side of the Isthmus of Panama and walked to the Pacific side to board another ship. However, during the walk, it was possible to contract many diseases, including yellow fever. Even though a railroad was built across the Isthmus in 1855, the threat of illness remained.

The land routes were just as hazardous, and yet many set out by wagon, by horse, and on foot. In their eagerness, they depended on poorly written guidebooks that often led to dangerous, even fatal, situations.

Because of the gold discoveries, California became a state on September 9, 1850. There was little in the way of an American government there. No one was prepared for all the people flooding into the new state. By the end of 1849, some 89,000 had reached California by both land and sea. Lawlessness was widespread. Many miners became discouraged when the gold proved so difficult to find.

The news went around the world. On almost every continent people jammed ships to reach California. Once there, sailors left their ships and joined the passengers to rush to the gold fields. The San Francisco anchorage was filled with abandoned ships. The pragmatic San Franciscans converted many of the ships into homes, hotels, and even a prison. Later, when they expanded the shoreline, they simply filled in the water around the ships. As a result, buried ships are still being unearthed today.

People around the world took part in the gold rush. Mexicans joined the local Hispanic population. Australians came in a sizable contingent, as did Europeans and South

Americans, especially Chileans. Southerners brought their slaves to the diggings as well.

When the miners came to California in 1849, prices for food shot through the roof. A single egg could cost up to three dollars and an onion two dollars.

Women were scarce in California at the time. However, the few women who made it to California were tough and resourceful. They founded many legitimate businesses and even prospected for gold. One even drove a stagecoach.

Only the Native Americans failed to profit from the gold rush. A disguised form of slavery begun by the Spanish missions continued, and Native American women and boys were sold into slavery until 1863. When Native Americans tried to protect themselves, they were killed — sometimes in wholesale massacres. Bounties were offered for their scalps. In both 1851 and 1852, bounty hunters were paid a total of one million dollars for the scalps of Native Americans.

A few Chinese had made their way to San Francisco before the gold rush. Life in China was very difficult; many were starving. Desperate for survival, people were willing to gamble their lives to reach California. By 1852, there were an estimated 25,000 Chinese there.

Originally, the Foreign Miners' Tax was aimed at all non-Americans, including Europeans. The license fee was set at twenty dollars a month, a high sum for many of the miners, who were barely surviving. Fights almost broke out between American and foreign miners over the tax. American merchants, afraid of losing so many foreign customers, protested. The fee was reduced, and eventually repealed.

However, by 1852, the tax was reenacted because of negative feelings against the Chinese miners. Though the fee was set at three dollars a month, it was now collected from only the Chinese. In 1853, the fee was raised to four dollars and in 1856 to six dollars.

Tax collectors were allowed to use force in order to obtain the money, part of which they kept. By 1862, eleven Chinese had been murdered by tax collectors. Only two collectors were ever convicted and hanged. Many districts gathered a large amount of money from the tax.

In early California, non-whites had no legal protection. In 1849, a law was passed that said, "No black or mulatto person or Indian shall be permitted to give evidence in favor of or against any white person." Soon the California courts included Chinese in the law and refused to accept their testimony as well.

An amazing amount of gold was found in California. In 1848, 11,866 troy ounces of gold were taken from the rivers and diggings at a value of $245,301. (There are twelve troy ounces to a pound.) In 1850, 1,996,586 troy ounces were taken, at a value of $41,273,106. The richest year of all time was 1852, with a total of 3,932,631 troy ounces at a value of $81,294,700.[1]

However, the gold was taken at an enormous cost to the environment. Even to this day, it has left what one geologist has called "moonscapes" where no plants can grow. Between 1854 and 1884, hydraulic mining shifted 1.5 billion cubic yards of debris, the same as digging eight Panama Canals. Much of that debris moved down the rivers, choking the bays. It has thickened the floor of San Francisco Bay by one to two yards.[2] Worse, quartz mining used mercury to extract the gold, poisoning the environment.

For better or worse, the California gold rush transformed many lives here and abroad. A few miners returned home rich, but far more found themselves poorer than ever. Many miners stayed in California and made their homes there. They returned to farm the rich fertile fields which they had once ignored in their hurry to reach the gold fields. Or they went to the cities to become mer-

1. *Gold Districts of California*, Bulletin 193, p. 4.
2. San Jose *Mercury News*, January 19, 1998, pp. 1A and 16A.

chants or start factories. They became doctors and engineers, bankers and lawyers, writers and artists. In short, they became the people who helped build California.

The Golden Mountain also forever changed the southern Chinese. They didn't need gold, just American money, so they found other work here in America. In increasingly troubled times, their remittances were able to keep their families alive back in China.

In an underpopulated state, these Chinese pioneers provided the raw, cheap labor that made California's factories and large farms possible. Without the Chinese, California could never have developed so fast. Later, the Chinese helped build the transcontinental railroad, joining the two coasts forever.

The gold rush changed how Americans dreamed. Before 1848, Americans went west for cheap land. After the gold rush, the West began to mean quick fortunes — whether it was in gold or oil or some other scheme.[3] And even today, California continues to draw people who see it as the place to make their dreams become reality.

3. J. S. Holliday, *The World Rushed In* (New York: Simon & Schuster, 1981).

After gold was discovered at John Sutter's sawmill, forty-five miles northeast of Sacramento, gold fever spread across the nation and around the world. California, once a thinly populated Mexican province, was soon flooded with doctors, lawyers, farmers, bakers, blacksmiths—all after the elusive gold nuggets. Tales of a Golden Mountain lured the Chinese, who sought their fortunes in the mines or as merchants.

Peasant gold-seekers crowded onto rustic ships and crossed over six thousand miles of the Pacific Ocean to reach their destination. Many men died during the dangerous months-long voyage.

San Francisco was the chief port for the gold seekers. Because there were no docks, ships anchored offshore in the harbor and passengers were ferried to shore in smaller boats. By 1851, over eight hundred ships clogged Yerba Buena Cove, top. When ships' crews left for the gold fields, the abandoned ships served as warehouses, saloons, stores, hotels, and prisons, bottom.

Prospectors traveled to stake their claims on the western slopes of the Sierra Nevadas. Laden with mining equipment, cooking gear, and other necessities, these men used a mule and a wagon to lighten the load.

Miners endured much hardship during their search for gold. When they reached the camps, they found back-breaking work in cold mountain streams, rampant disease, and high prices. Meals often consisted of only rice and beans, sometimes with salt pork, hardtack, and jerked beef. Miners slept outside or in tents, but those who planned to stay longer built cabins.

207

Sacramento's crucial position at the junction of the Sacramento and American rivers made it a major supply center vital to miners and merchants.

This Mormon Island Emporium's broadside advertises "China Preserves" and "China Bread and Cakes" along with shovels, picks, and axes. The store also served as a mail and banking center.

Langton & Bro's Express in Downieville, California, weighed and purchased gold dust from miners.

Early in the Gold Rush, Americans happily worked side by side with foreigners. But after 1850, as gold became more difficult to find and prejudices grew, people from Asia, Europe, Mexico, and South America were banned from some camps. Some felt that the gold found in California belonged solely to American citizens.

For protection against prejudiced bullies, Chinese established their own mining camps, succeeding where others had failed. While some lived in prefabricated houses that they'd brought from China, others lived in tents.

A Chinese man uses an abacus to balance accounts in the office of a mercantile house in San Francisco. He records the figures in traditional calligraphy, using a brush and ink.

The rocker, or cradle, is a wooden box, open at one end and closed at the other. Miners shoveled sand into the rocker and poured water over it. When it is rocked back and forth, the sand and water leave the rocker, and the gold is caught on the rocker's cleats.

A young Chinese miner with his rocker moves to a fresh claim.

After the Gold Rush was over, Chinese who had once been miners were forced to look for other employment. They provided the cheap labor for California's factories and large farms, which allowed for the state's rapid development. Others became merchants, such as these men in a San Francisco butcher shop.

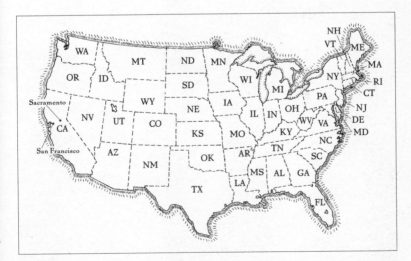

Modern map of the United States, showing the locations of San Francisco and Sacramento, California.

About the Author

◈ ◈ ◈

As a child growing up in California, Laurence Yep couldn't help hearing about the gold rush. He says, "When I was young, I thought of the gold rush as a glorious, fun-filled treasure hunt. However, when I grew older and learned more, I realized that the gold rush was an even bigger story. It drew dreamers from around the world. So the story is not just the dreams of one person or of one group but of the entire world.

"The gold rush also had a serious, dangerous side. The miners brought not only their dreams but their prejudices, too. And greed sharpened those prejudices so that they had a deadly, violent edge. Because of that, the gold rush is not only a story of dreams but of shadowy, frightening nightmares."

Laurence Yep is a respected author of historical fiction for young readers. He is the author of two Newbery Honor books: *Dragonwings* and *Dragon's Gate*. For *Dragonwings*, he won the IRA Children's Writing Award, the Carter G. Woodson Award, and the Phoenix Award. *Dragon's Gate* was awarded the Commonwealth Club Award and the Beatty Award from the California Librarian's Association. His other awards include the *Boston Globe-Horn Book* Award and the Jane Addams Peace Award for *Child of the Owl* and the Christopher Medal for *Star Fisher.*

Laurence Yep has been a National Endowment for the Arts fellow and a writer-in-residence at the University of California, Santa Barbara. He lives in Pacific Grove, California, with his wife, writer Joanne Ryder.

To H. Mark Lai,
a pioneer in his own right

Acknowledgments

The author would like to thank the California Historical Society, the Oakland Museum, the California Railroad Museum, the Bancroft Library, the Monterey Public Library, and the McHenry Library at the University of California, Santa Cruz, for their help with this book. He would also like to thank his long-suffering wife, Joanne Ryder, who was such a good sport while he obsessed about the research.

Grateful acknowledgment is made for permission to reprint the following:

Cover portrait: National Archives - Pacific Division.

Cover background: Gold mining in California, lithograph, 1871, by Currier & Ives, The Granger Collection.

Page 205 (top): "Emigrants leaving China for California," from *Why and How*, by Russell H. Conwell (Boston, 1871). California Historical Society, FN-01002.

Page 205 (bottom): Chinese emigrating to America, *Harper's Weekly*.

Page 206 (top): Yerba Buena Cove, California Historical Society FN-15618.

Page 206 (bottom): Ships beached as buildings, The Bancroft Library, University of California, Berkeley.

Page 207 (top): Miners, North Wind Picture Archives.

Page 207 (bottom): Miners in front of their cabin, Collection of W. Bruce Lundberg.

Page 208 (top): Sacramento street scene, *The American West in the Nineteenth Century*, Dover Publications, Inc., New York, 1992.

Page 208 (bottom): Advertisement, The Bancroft Library, University of California, Berkeley.

Page 209: Langton & Bro's, Collection of the Society of California Pioneers.

Page 210 (top): Chinese man being attacked, New York Public Library.

Page 210 (bottom): Chinese mining camp, *The American West in the Nineteenth Century*, Dover Publications, Inc., New York, 1992.

Page 211 (top): Man balancing accounts, Culver Pictures.

Page 211 (bottom): Miner with rocker, The Bancroft Library, University of California, Berkeley.

Page 212: Chinese miner, Nevada Historical Society.

Page 213 (top): Chinese butcher shop, Wyland Stanley Collection, photograph by I.W. Taber; courtesy of The Bancroft Library, University of California, Berkeley.

Page 213 (bottom): Map by Heather Saunders.

Other books in the My Name Is America series

The Journal of Ben Uchida
Citizen 13559, Mirror Lake Internment Camp
by Barry Denenberg

The Journal of William Thomas Emerson
A Revolutionary War Patriot
by Barry Denenberg

The Journal of Sean Sullivan
A Transcontinental Railroad Worker
by William Durbin

The Journal of James Edmond Pease
A Civil War Union Soldier
by Jim Murphy

The Journal of Joshua Loper
A Black Cowboy
by Walter Dean Myers

The Journal of Scott Pendleton Collins
A World War II Soldier
by Walter Dean Myers

The Journal of Jasper Jonathan Pierce
A Pilgrim Boy
by Ann Rinaldi

While the events described and some of the characters in this book may be
based on actual historical events and real people, Wong Ming-Chung
is a fictional character, created by the author, and his journal
and its epilogue are works of fiction.

The display type is set in Humana Serif.
The text type is set in Berling Roman.
Book design by Elizabeth B. Parisi.
Photo research by Zoe Moffitt and Pamela Heller.

ISBN 0-439-56713-0

2 3 4 5 6 7 ·8 9 10   40   12 11 10 09 08 07 06 05 04